Reverend Colt

Paul Colten and his wife Christina had moved West with dreams that were different from most settlers. Paul was a preacher who regarded the frontier as a place in great spiritual need, but when a man the pastor had tried to help murdered Christina, Colten's idealism died amidst gunsmoke. He went after the killer and took the first step in becoming the gunfighter known as Reverend Colt.

Arriving in Grayson to kill a man for money, he finds a town under the brutal control of a wealthy rancher, Leonard Caldwell. Colt befriends a former lawman whose badge was snatched away by Caldwell and finds himself in sympathy with a young couple who run the local newspaper. The *Grayson Herald* is printing the truth about recent killings in the town at great personal risk.

Colt admires those who are standing against corruption, but the gunfighter realizes that the brutal men who rule Grayson will not be stopped by newspaper editorials alone. Reverend Colt's skills with a gun will be put to the ultimate test.

Reverend Colt

James Clay

ISBN 978-0-7198-1180-7

Robert Hale Limited
Clerkenwell House
Clerkenwell Green
London EC1R 0HT

www.halebooks.com

For Jeanine and Andrew:
two buckaroos who ride the waves

Typeset by
Derek Doyle & Associates, Shaw Heath
Printed and bound in Great Britain by
CPI Antony Rowe, Chippenham and Eastbourne

CHAPTER ONE

The box wagon marked *Brother Joseph's Traveling Wonders* made a succession of noisy rattles as it moved toward Grayson, Texas. The road was rutted but not dusty. Mandy Woods plucked at a guitar and enjoyed the breeze that danced on her dark-brown hair.

'So, Dad, we'll sell the elixir after "Oh Suzanna". After that, we'll close with "Swing Low, Sweet Chariot". How does that sound to you?'

'Why, just fine.' Joseph Woods smiled at his daughter, who was sitting next to him as he directed the wagon's four horses. A few years ago folks were calling Mandy 'cute'. Now, at eighteen, they were using the word 'beautiful'.

Joe was proud of his daughter, but ashamed of himself. Mandy had a real knack for music, but she was completely self-taught. He should have gotten her into a fine school somewhere. Joe Woods pressed his lips together and shook his head at that fanciful notion. The proprietor of *Brother Joseph's Traveling Wonders* had enough trouble just living from one meal to the next.

'We should do very well in Grayson.' Mandy sounded excited. 'There will be lots of people there for the celebration.'

Lots of men, her father thought. That's what bothered him the most. Joseph Woods knew too much about men to believe they gathered around the wagon only to enjoy his daughter's singing. Her wholesome charm quickly captivated them, however, and they good-naturedly bought bottles of the elixir after she extolled its virtues.

Joseph Woods looked at the rough ground that moved under him. He was using his daughter's beauty to scratch out a living selling snake oil. What kind of a man would do such a thing?

Gunshots interrupted his musings. Two riders approached the wagon from the direction of Grayson, firing into the air. Joseph Woods halted the wagon, relaxing a little as the two men holstered their pistols. 'Afternoon, gents, what's up?'

'Davin and me heard you two was comin' into town tonight for the celebration.' As the man spoke his eyes were admiring Mandy.

'Yeah,' his partner proclaimed. 'Mr Caldwell hisself sent us out ta meet ya and give ya an escort inta town.'

They were lying and Joe Woods knew it. The riders had stopped near the wagon's two lead horses, one on each side. The first man who spoke was tall and heavyset. His partner, Davin, was almost as tall, but thin, with a swollen upper lip that formed a half-moon over a mouth with only a scattering of teeth.

Woods decided to try playing along with the deception. 'We sure appreciate the thoughtfulness, gents. But, you know, we've driven this trail many times. Don't need any help. You can get on with your business.'

'I think we may have ourselfs some interestin' business right here.' The heavy-set man hadn't stopped looking at Mandy. 'My name is Ollie, sweet thang. We sure did enjoy your singin' last time you was in town. Yeah, we enjoyed it a lot.'

'You men have stopped this wagon long enough.' Joseph Woods's voice was low and angry. 'We've got—'

Mandy placed a calming hand on her father's arm and

6

smiled at the newcomers. 'I'm learning a new song; could I audition it for you?' She turned up the smile a fraction. ' "Audition" means to sing a song to find out if folks like it. Could you let me try the song out on you?'

The two saddletramps looked at each other and shared a guffaw. 'Why sure, sweet thang,' Ollie said. 'Davin and me would be right honored to be the first ones to hear your new song.'

'Thanks!' Mandy hurriedly strummed her fingers across the guitar strings and stood up. 'I sing this song with a banjo; it's right behind me.' She placed the guitar down, grabbed a Winchester, which lay behind the seat, and pointed it at the newcomers. 'You men ride off. Now!'

Ollie and Davin laughed once again.

'My daughter is a good shot!' Joe Woods yelled. 'We'd have starved if not for all those rabbits she's brought down, and you two are a lot bigger than rabbits. Better do what she says!'

Mandy's entire body was shaking. Her father was telling the truth, but shooting men was a lot different from shooting rabbits. Could she kill a human being?

'I don't believe ya, mister.' Davin stared at the rifle, which was pointed at him. 'I say that's jus' a play gun that pwetty little chickie carved from a piece of wood.'

Mandy hastily held the Winchester out in front of her. 'This rifle is real and you'd better start riding—'

'Yaaaa!' Ollie yelled, and slapped the rump of one of the lead horses. Davin followed his example and the two horses moved forward a step, causing the wagon to lurch. Mandy fell to the ground, managing to hold on to the Winchester with one hand.

The young woman scrambled to her feet, but Ollie had hastily dismounted and grabbed the Winchester before she had a chance to point it at him. Both Mandy and her attacker now had their hands on the gun and they began a bizarre dance as each tried to wrestle the weapon from the other. A gleeful, excited laugh cut the air as Davin came running to help his partner.

'Let go of the rifle, sweet thang,' Ollie's voice was threatening, 'or I may have to put some bruises on that pretty face of yours.'

Joe Woods frantically searched behind the wagon's seat for the Colt Peacemaker he thought was there. He cursed himself in a low whisper. '. . . must have left the thing in the wagon. Some help I am.'

Joseph jumped from the wagon and hit the ground in time to intercept Davin. He faked a punch to Davin's head, then tripped him. Ollie freed the rifle from Mandy and swung it at her father as Davin hit the ground. Joe jack knifed in time to miss the blow, then landed a hard punch to Ollie's midriff. 'Run, Mandy, run!'

Mandy ran toward a grove of trees. She quickly glanced backwards and saw that Davin was back on his feet and fighting with her father. Ollie was taking off after her. The young woman had been sure something like this would happen. Her running off would divide the two attackers. She hoped her father could handle Davin, but had no idea what she'd do about Ollie. The Winchester, which Ollie now carried with him, didn't make her predicament any easier.

Joseph lacerated his opponent with several short, hard punches. Davin again dropped to the ground and Joseph hastily reached down and jerked the Remington from the fallen man's holster.

'You's jus' lucky, ol' man.' Davin caressed the right side of his face, humiliated to have been bested by a man at least twenty years his senior.

Joseph started to say something but was stopped by his daughter's scream. He turned and began to run toward the grove of trees. A shot sounded behind him and a bullet glanced off the heel of one of his boots, causing him to stumble. The Remington flew from his hand as he instinctively threw out his arms to break the fall.

'I'll show ya, ol' man.' Davin carried a small pistol, which he had snatched from his boot. He moved quickly toward Joseph, intent on killing the man who had bested him.

Another scream sounded from the grove of trees. 'I'm her only hope,' Joe Woods whispered to himself. He glanced at the Remington, which lay about five feet away from him, and made a fast dive for it.

A strange cacophony of sounds suddenly resounded in Joseph's ear. He heard a pounding of hoofbeats, a gunshot and a man's loud cry. As he grabbed the Remington he glanced backwards and saw Davin drop to the ground.

Shifting his glance, Joseph saw a man astride a strawberry roan, wearing a black frock coat. The look on his face was grim as he returned a Colt .45 to its holster.

'My daughter!' Joe pointed toward the trees. The stranger turned the roan and rode hard.

Mandy screamed as she ran between the trees, hoping to tire out her pursuer, but she realized that her efforts were futile. Ollie was laughing and enjoying the chase. Maybe she could climb one of the trees, but the branches were so high, it would take her too long to reach the first one. Ollie could easily pull her down. A small stream fronted the trees but it was too shallow for swimming.

A shot resounded from the area where the wagon had stopped. Without thinking, the young woman immediately halted and looked back. 'Dad!'

Ollie had been closer than Mandy realized. He lurched from behind a cottonwood, grabbed the woman's right arm, and dragged her toward the stream as she made a loud cry. They were clear of the trees when Mandy saw that her captor still had the Winchester in his right hand. She took a hard swing with her free arm, landing a fist against Ollie's mouth, just as a second shot scorched the air, followed by a man's painful wail. The cry didn't sound like her father's voice, but Mandy couldn't be sure.

Ollie let go of the girl, shouting a string of obscenities, then tossed the rifle to the ground and made a fast sprint to grab her, this time with both hands. Mandy managed a few kicks to Ollie's shins but the large man overpowered her. He ripped the young woman's blouse and pushed her to the ground. 'Playtime is over, sweet thang.'

'True enough.' The man in the frock coat stepped quickly from the trees. 'Stay right where you are, Ollie.'

Keeping his eyes on Ollie, the stranger took a few steps toward Mandy as he took off his coat and handed it to her. 'Are you OK?'

'Yes.' She hastily put on the coat.

'You're quite the gent, for a man who kills for money.' Ollie tried to sound tough but couldn't keep the quiver from his voice.

'I just killed your partner and didn't get a dime for it.' The newcomer took several steps away from the woman. 'I'll gladly see to it that you join him and I won't charge a penny for the service.'

As he talked, the newcomer made a gesture toward Mandy, indicating that she should back away. The woman hastily got to her feet and put more distance between her and the two men. As she did so, she noticed that Ollie's tormentor wore a Colt .45, its holster tied down on his right leg.

'So, Reverend Colt.' Ollie's voice resounded with mockery. 'Why do you wanna kill me?'

'You and Davin are liars.' There wasn't a hint of reassurance in the cold smile that Reverend Colt gave his opponent. 'You two snakes convinced me that you had nothing to do with rustling cattle from your boss. You were just fun-loving saddle-tramps who got fooled by a crooked ramrod.'

A look of desperation came over Ollie's face. 'That was true—'

'I've heard what you two have been doing for the last year or so.'

'You here for revenge?'

'No, just happened along. But it is always nice to clear up unfinished business. Take off your holster, Ollie, and drop it, gently, to the ground.'

Ollie's face reflected both fear and confusion. His eyes darted toward the girl, who was now looking on the scene with a quiet confidence. Ollie no longer had sway over her and felt humiliated because of it. Still, he wasn't about to get himself killed over that humiliation.

The saddletramp unbuckled his holster and tossed it to the ground. Maybe he could talk his way out of this. 'Don't it say somethin' in the Good Book 'bout forgivin' people?'

'Yes.' Colt picked up Ollie's gun and pointed it at him. 'To be specific, Scripture says we should forgive our brother on seventy times seven occasions.' Colt shook his head. 'Afraid I'm not quite there yet, Ollie. One time is all I can give you. It's a shame you didn't make better use of it.'

Colt shifted his gaze to the sound of hasty footsteps. Joseph Woods came running into the clearing, then sprinted toward his daughter and embraced her.

'Are you. . . ?' Joe looked uneasily at the frock coat.

'I'm fine, Dad, just fine.' She sighed deeply as her father released his hold, then nodded toward Colt. 'The Rev . . . ah . . . gentleman who lent me his coat was able to, ah, set matters right.'

Father and daughter approached Colt, ignoring his captive, who now stood with his face toward the ground. 'Sir, we're beholden to you. My name is Joseph Woods and this here is my daughter, Mandy.'

'My name is Paul Colten.' He smiled and touched two fingers to his hat. 'I've sort of picked up the name Reverend Colt.'

Mandy Woods gazed at her rescuer. He was a tall, well-built man, sandy-haired with an angular face and a mustache that was thick but not bushy.

'Are you a real preacher?' she asked.

'I was.' A darkness came over Paul Colten's face, and there was a moment of awkward silence. Then, Colten smiled and a cheeriness returned to his voice. 'Sir, you probably saw my horse; it's tied along the first row of trees. Why don't you and Miss Woods ride him back to the road?' Colt's eyes darted to the rifle lying on the ground. 'That Winchester belong to you?'

'Yes,' Joseph Woods replied quickly. 'And please, call me Joe.'

'Be sure and take the Winchester with you, Joe. You never know when you might encounter some snakes. Meanwhile, Ollie and I can catch up on old times as we walk back.'

Colt and his prisoner walked in silence until they arrived at Colt's roan, which had been tethered to a scraggly tree at the side of the road. The box wagon stood a short distance away. 'Time to add a little something to your wardrobe, Ollie.' Paul Colten took a rope from his saddle and tied the outlaw's hands behind his back. After testing his handiwork with the rope, Colt emptied Ollie's Army .44 and placed the gun in one of the saddle-bags on his strawberry roan.

Holding the rope in his hand, Colt continued his walk toward *Brother Joseph's Traveling Wonders* with Ollie clomping beside him like an exhausted mule.

Mandy stepped out of the wagon wearing a different blouse and carrying Colt's frock coat. She gingerly hopped off the small ladder that leaned against the back of the wagon and approached the two men.

'Thank you.' She smiled shyly at Colt as she handed him his coat.

Paul Colten returned the smile but said nothing as he slipped it back on, keeping a close watch on Ollie.

The young woman nodded her head to the left. 'My father is digging a grave to bury . . . his name is Davin, isn't it?'

Mandy looked directly at the man who had attacked her. Ollie seemed startled and oddly moved by the gesture, like a small boy who had been reprimanded, then given a few words of encouragement by his teacher.

'Yeah, that's his name. Davin.'

Mandy headed for the gravesite and the two men followed her. Colt had originally planned to bind Ollie completely and toss him into the back of the wagon for the remainder of the trip. But the young lady obviously believed that the man Colt had just killed needed a proper burial first. He couldn't argue with her. Still, the sudden observance of propriety made him a touch uneasy.

At the gravesite, Colt tied Ollie's feet before helping Joe to dig the hole deep enough to keep the corpse safe from coyotes. After they were finished, Colt again freed up Ollie's ankles. A moment of uncertain silence followed as everyone's eyes shifted to Davin's body, which was wrapped in an old brown blanket.

'Could I see his face? Jus' one more time?' Ollie asked.

Colt quickly walked to the corpse, stooped over and pulled the blanket back to reveal Davin's face.

Ollie stared down and spoke softly. 'He wasn't much of a man. Guess I ain't, either. But he was my friend. Ain't had many of those, probably never have another.' Ollie inhaled deeply and looked away. 'So long, pard.'

Colt pulled the blanket back over Davin's face. As he did so, Paul Colten saw the expression in Mandy Woods's eyes; she was feeling sympathy for a man who, only a short time before, had tried to brutally assault her. Colten admired the young woman and felt regret for something he had long ago lost.

'You still carry a Good Book in your saddle-bags?'

Ollie's question jerked Colten from some private thoughts. 'Yes.'

'Before we bury him could you read some words? Something sorta pretty?'

'Of course.' The reply was casual, but Colt felt a deep sense of confusion and resentment. A worthless, no-good thug had put him in a position where he would have to read aloud passages dealing with mercy and forgiveness, passages that brought him no comfort, only torment.

Colt glanced toward his roan. He took his gun from its holster and handed it to Joseph Woods. 'Remember what this man almost did to your daughter. If he tries anything at all, kill him.'

Then Reverend Colt went to get his Bible.

CHAPTER TWO

'Yep, Ox, when I was at the *New York Courier* I reported on just about everything. Even did theater reviews. That was my downfall. I ripped apart an actress who played Ophelia in a production of *Hamlet*. Madeline Brinthrope was her name and I didn't care if she was the publisher's daughter. She was a lousy actress and that's what I wrote in my review. Cost me my job, but I kept my integrity. That's what counts.'

'You're right about that, Phineas.' The bartender sounded genuinely impressed. 'I mean the integrity and all. Why, you've never once asked for a free drink. You always pay. Like another?'

'No, thanks.' the young man placed his glass back down on the bar. He felt that Ox didn't really grasp the full importance of his journalistic integrity, but decided to hold off on any further elaboration. 'I have to keep a clear head. This is a busy time for a newspaper man.' Phineas liked to refer to himself as a newspaper man. He had given up on 'journalist'. The folks in Grayson, Texas just laughed at that.

'Yeah, it would be a busy time for me, too, if I was still the deputy sheriff. I miss bein' a lawdog.'

'You're not doing so bad, Ox. I mean tending bar, and other stuff.'

'There's a lot of other stuff. I'm a part-time barkeep at Mr Hayworth's two saloons and I hafta keep the places lookin' decent. Also gotta keep tabs on his livery. Course, men will always want to drink and the livery will always need cleanin' out. Guess I got a job with a future.'

Phineas had little concern about Ox's future but was interested in his name. 'How'd you get the nickname, "Ox"?' His voice was artificially casual.

'Had it so long, can't remember.' One look at Ox would partially answer the question. He was a huge man, well over six feet and heavyset. 'Why d'ya ask?'

'Just making conversation.' Phineas looked about nervously, then nodded at the bartender. 'Better get going. The sheriff said he needed to see me about something important.'

Phineas Wilsey hurried out of the saloon feeling embarrassed over his question. Since he was a boy, the reporter had been trying to replace 'Phineas' with a nickname. He had tried 'Buck', 'Rock', Flash', and would even have settled for 'Phin', but nothing took hold.

As he shuffled down the boardwalk, Phineas reminded himself that he was one of the few men in town who didn't carry a gun. That was certainly appropriate. As owner and editor of the *Grayson Herald*, it was his responsibility to bring civility and integrity to a wild, untamed land.

A bothersome thought began to itch in the young man's mind. He had polished the truth a tad in regard to what he told Ox about his review of *Hamlet*. In fact, he had not known that Madeline Brinthrope was the publisher's daughter, a fact that his boss had found to be incredible.

'You bonehead,' the red-faced editor had shouted at him. 'Every day it reads on the mast of this paper, "An independent journal owned by the Brinthrope family". How many Brinthrope families can there be?!'

'Well. . . .' was all Phineas could stammer.

'Get out of my sight! I never want to see you again!'

Phineas paused and pondered what he had just been told. 'Ah, does this mean I'm fired?'

At that point his boss's voice had become so high-pitched and fierce that Phineas couldn't make out exactly what he was saying. But the young journalist had no trouble getting the drift. On his way out of the Courier building, an older colleague had put a hand on Phineas's right shoulder and advised, 'Go West, young man! Nobody in the East will have anything to do with you.'

Sheriff Louis Dixon was cleaning a gun when Phineas stepped into his office. 'Thought I'd stop by, Lou.'

'Why?' Lou Dixon was obviously irritated by the informality of the peach-faced kid from New York.

'Remember, we passed on the boardwalk earlier today and you—'

'Oh yeah.' Dixon got up from his desk, stretched, then ran a hand through his black mustache and beard. 'Look, tonight is something special. This town has been around for ten years. As you know, we're havin' a sort of birthday celebration.'

'Yes.'

'Now, there's goin' to be a lot of hoorawin'. Some fools will probably get shot before the night's over. Mr Caldwell wants none of that stuff in the newspaper. You just write about what's proper – the speeches, that sort of thing.'

'Right.'

'And Mr Caldwell says—'

The door to the office opened and Paul Colten walked in with a hand firmly around Ollie's left arm. Ollie's hands were still tied and Colten still held the rope. Joseph and Mandy Woods followed behind.

'Well, well, Ollie, what have you been up to now?' the sheriff asked.

Colt spoke. 'Ollie and his partner, Davin, attacked a wagon being driven by these two people.'

Dixon looked at Joseph Woods and his daughter. 'You two have been in town before. You sell some phony—'

'Sir—'

Colt interrupted Mandy. 'These folks were coming into town to provide entertainment for the festivities tonight. Ollie and Davin stopped them.'

The moment Mandy entered the office, Phineas had taken off his large Stetson, smiled, and nodded in a courtly manner. Mandy hadn't noticed him. He had continued to look in the young lady's direction as often as propriety would allow. Finally, while Colt was explaining what had occurred at the edge of town, Mandy's eyes fused with those of the reporter. Phineas made a slight bow and, as he had often seen men do in the West, he raised two fingers to touch his hat, forgetting that he had taken off the Stetson, which was now in his left hand. Mandy responded with a slight smile, then turned to face the sheriff.

Dixon shrugged his shoulders before speaking. 'Well, you got Davin buried and, from what you say, ah, what's your name?'

'Paul Colten.'

Dixon paused and carefully assessed the man in front of him. 'You the one they call Reverend Colt?'

Colt nodded his head.

Dixon's eyes held a lot of questions but he didn't ask any of them. 'The way I see it, Reverend Colt, Ollie never had a chance to do any real harm. There's a big night ahead. Don't see why I should crowd up a jail cell. After all, they didn't really attack the wagon. Joe Woods stopped on his own.'

Mandy Woods had been in Grayson enough times to understand how the town worked. 'But they lied to us, Sheriff. They said they had been sent out by Mr Caldwell.'

Dixon's eyes flared with anger as he looked at Ollie. 'You stupid fool! Mr Caldwell is the wealthiest rancher in this area. He'd never stoop to hiring worthless saddletramps! Maybe there's room for you in the jail after all.'

Colt hurriedly untied the outlaw's hands. As the sheriff escorted Ollie through a door that led to the cells, Colt spoke to Mandy and Joseph. 'You'll need to hang around a few more minutes to—'

'Excuse me, folks, my name is Phineas Wilsey. I couldn't help overhearing your conversation with Sheriff Dixon.' He gave Joseph a quick glance and then looked at Mandy. 'I gather that you two are in the theater,' Phineas turned to Colt, 'and that you, sir, are a man of the cloth.'

'Well. . . .'

Apparently not noticing that Colt had begun to speak, Phineas continued. 'The theater and the church, two institutions that are desperately needed in this wild, untamed land.' He tried to gauge how the young lady was responding to his words. She seemed more confused than impressed but he plowed on. 'Please rest assured that as editor and chief reporter for this town's newspaper, I will assist you in any way I can.'

Colt took a deep breath and figured he had done about all he could for Mandy and Joseph Woods. He had helped them with two violent saddletramps, but when it came to Phineas they were on their own. He hastily excused himself and left the office.

CHAPTER THREE

Two well-dressed men stood in the middle of Grayson's main street. They inhaled, held themselves upright and motionless and tried to look distinguished. To most people passing by on the boardwalk, they looked either grim or ridiculous.

'Got it!' Phineas Wilsey shouted and stepped around from behind his camera. 'Thank you, gentlemen. I'd like to get one more picture. This time with your hats off.'

The shorter of the two men glanced at his companion to observe his reaction to the request. The taller man didn't glance back, not caring what Mayor Horatio Camrose wanted to do.

'One more picture will be fine, Phineas, but try not to take too much time,' said Leonard Caldwell.

'I'll work as fast as I can, sir.' Phineas began to fuss with his apparatus, then paused. 'Ah, Mr Caldwell?'

'Yes?'

'Do you think maybe this time you and the mayor could smile for the picture? I think people might—'

'Phineas, you take the picture. I will decide the pose.'

'Yes, sir.'

Mayor Camrose had smiled and nodded his head at Phineas's suggestion. He quickly dropped the smile and took on a serious demeanor, relieved that Leonard Caldwell had not witnessed his faux pas.

The rancher squinted in Phineas's direction. 'I've never seen a camera like that one.'

The newspaper man proudly patted the brown, wooden object that sat on a tripod. 'It's the latest thing from New York, a Pearsall, designed to take pictures of baseball games, but it works fine for my purposes.'

Caldwell nodded, then looked behind him at Horatio Camrose. 'Your Honor, I see they have completed the platform for tonight. While our young friend gets ready for the next picture, let's go over and have a look at it.'

'Excellent suggestion, Leonard.' There was a touch of nervous uncertainty in the mayor's voice. Caldwell wanted to get him out of earshot of the photographer. This chat wasn't going to be pleasant.

The rancher spoke in a hearty voice as the two men walked toward the platform. 'It'll be a grand celebration tonight, Horatio.'

'Thanks to your generosity, Leonard, and I will personally make sure everyone in town is aware—'

Caldwell motioned backwards with his head. 'I have a newspaper man who takes care of that.' He paused and lowered his voice before changing the subject. 'But no matter what the newspaper reports, Stephen Hayworth won't be very impressed. No, he won't be grateful at all, even though the celebration will help business at his saloons and probably at his livery too.'

'Stephen Hayworth is just one man, there's no reason—'

Leonard Caldwell's voice once again boomed as the two men reached the small platform, which was head height. 'Looks pretty solid to me, Horatio. I think it will be able to hold the two of us for fifteen minutes, don't you?'

'Yes, Leonard.'

Caldwell ran his hand over the wood and again lowered his voice. 'He's a strange bird, that Hayworth. I'd be willing to bet there's something dishonest about the way he acquired his businesses. Maybe you should look into the paperwork, Horatio. You might find that Stephen Hayworth is a crook.'

'There's no way I can—' Camrose's eyes went wide as his companion brought a fist down on the platform.

'Horatio, you are the town's mayor and only lawyer. I expect good work from you.'

'Yes, of course, but. . . .'

A smile came across Caldwell's face, but there was no mirth in it. 'Of course, you haven't always been our only lawyer. I remember a year or so ago when a young man came into Grayson and hung out his shingle. Was a hard-working barrister, from what I hear. I believe he was taking some business away from you. Yes, quite a bit of business.'

'Please. . . .'

'Our photographer is ready for us, Horatio! We'd better get back.'

As the two men strolled back toward Phineas Wilsey, Caldwell continued to taunt the mayor. 'Yes, that young lawyer did a terrific job, but this Texas heat must have gotten to him. He started talking about men beating him up. Why, as I recall he even accused our sheriff and his deputy of doing the dastardly deed.'

Leonard Caldwell gave a loud, theatrical laugh, then continued. 'Can you imagine fine men like Lou Dixon and Harry Blackburn doing such a thing?'

'Leonard, I don't want—'

The two men stopped talking as they were once again in range of the camera. Caldwell quickly lifted his right palm and then dropped it. 'Of course, Horatio, why talk about such unpleasant matters? Besides, it makes no difference now. That young man rode out of town one morning and hasn't been seen since.'

The rancher looked toward Phineas. 'Are you ready?'

'Yes, sir.'

Caldwell and the mayor once again stood erect, this time holding their hats in front of them. There was another shout of 'Got it,' and the two men began to breathe again.

'Yes, you've been a very fortunate man, Horatio,' Caldwell said as he put his hat back on. 'I just hope your good luck continues.'

'Yes, well. . . .'

'I won't keep you any longer. I know you have a lot of work to do.'

Mayor Horatio Camrose knew a dismissal when he heard one. He bade his companion a respectful goodbye and hurried off.

Leonard Caldwell walked briskly toward the newspaper man, who was carefully attending to his camera. 'So, Phineas, will the picture of his Honor and myself be published in the paper?'

'Yes, sir,' came the fast reply. 'It will be an historic event. Thanks to the equipment you helped purchase, the *Grayson Herald* will be the first newspaper west of New York City to include a photograph in one of its editions!' Phineas couldn't be sure of his assertion about being the first paper outside of New York to run a picture but it sounded good, and there was little chance that Leonard Caldwell would actually look into it.

'Fine, fine. Are you taking any more pictures for the paper?'

'I am taking more pictures, but not for the paper.'

'Then, why are you taking them?'

'Why, for posterity, Mr Caldwell. Years from now people will want to see what Grayson, Texas looked like on its tenth anniversary.'

The rancher's face crunched up then fell back into place. 'Yes, I suppose so, but don't take any pictures of the two saloons or Hayworth's livery.'

'But sir—'

'I don't think posterity will be very interested in Stephen Hayworth's saloons or livery, do you?'

'No, Mr Caldwell, of course not.'

CHAPTER FOUR

Reverend Colt looked down on the main street of Grayson from his second-floor hotel room. He had taken a bath and had a quick meal, but he still didn't feel refreshed.

'Should have stopped being naïve long ago,' Colt spoke quietly to himself as he thought about the events of the day. Davin had almost killed Joseph Woods and there could be no doubt as to what Ollie had in mind for Mandy Woods. How many times had those two worthless men gotten away with harming others?

He could have had them jailed over a year ago, but he had listened to their appeals to his compassionate side. 'Won't happen again,' they'd said with conviction.

Outside, a platform had been constructed for a ceremony that was to kick off the town's tenth birthday celebration. Colt watched as two men stepped onto the platform amid loud cheers from the crowd. The cheers were aimed more at the setting sun than at the two gentlemen. The desk clerk at the hotel had informed Colt that there would be a short ceremony before the festivities got started with a fireworks display.

The two men now on the platform were a curious contrast. Both appeared to be in their fifties, but one was short and portly while the other was tall and muscular, with leathery skin that came from spending long hours in the sun.

There were enough kerosene lanterns hanging nearby that both men were clearly visible to the crowd. The portly man seemed to instinctively find the most well-lit part of the platform as he began to address the crowd. From what Colt could hear the speaker was the town's mayor and his Honor knew where the real power in the town resided. The mayor kept assuring the town folks that none of the good things that were happening that night would have been possible without Leonard Caldwell.

About every third line the mayor employed led to applause from the crowd and a smiling nod from the tall man on the platform, who was obviously Leonard Caldwell. Then the mayor stepped aside and allowed the real boss to take center stage.

Caldwell took off a bowler he was wearing and ran a hand over his bald head, obviously making a joke about his lack of hair. Then he held both hands up high as if being robbed and shouted, 'Let the celebration begin!'

Colt watched the start of the fireworks display from his window. It did nothing to dispel his grim mood. As he left his room, he reflected on the fact that he had killed a man that day. He wondered how many more he would have to kill before completing the job he had to do in Grayson, Texas.

With most of the town watching the fireworks, Colt decided to make a quick stop at the Mule Kick. The place would soon be filled with celebrators. Now was the time for a beer.

Inside, the saloon was almost empty. Two men sat at a round table with a bottle between them. They looked at Colt with a harsh mockery that came from more than a few drinks.

One man was leaning against the bar. Colt recognized him from his stop at the town's livery. The man's name was Skeeter. Skeeter's pleadings with the bartender could be heard even above the fireworks.

'Please, George, just one more.'

'Now, Skeeter, you've had your two drinks.' The bartender was a tall young man whose thinning hair made him look older than his actual years.

'But I can pay ya!'

'Skeeter, we both work for the same man. Mr Hayworth has handed down strict orders: "Serve Skeeter two drinks, but no more."'

'But tonight's special, lots of celebratin' and—'

George's voice became louder; he was growing weary of this encounter. 'You know, there are some people who claim you should make a drunk give up the booze completely. You oughta be glad the boss man doesn't see it that way.'

'Hey, George, that ain't a nice way to talk to a customer!' One of the two men who had been sharing a bottle was now on his feet, the bottle in his hand. His skin was sallow and doughy, reflecting a life spent largely in saloons. 'Look what I'm gonna do for ya, Skeeter.' He took a few steps and placed the bottle on an empty table, then returned to his companion. 'Why, Amos and me was just gettin' started on that bottle. There's plenty there to enjoy. Help yourself.'

Skeeter looked uncertain and a little frightened. 'That's nice of ya, Mitch.'

Mitch remained standing near the table where Amos sat with only two empty glasses in front of him. 'Like you said, Skeeter, this is a celebration time.' He pointed at the bottle. 'So, start celebratin'.'

Skeeter had taken three steps toward the bottle when a shot exploded in front of him. The livery man jumped back, crying out in fright.

Mitch guffawed loudly, and held up the gun that was now in his right hand. 'I surely do apologize, Skeeter. Guess my gun must have gone off accidental, like. You just try again. Maybe you can make it to the bottle this time.'

Skeeter stared at Mitch for a few moments, then looked straight ahead at the prize that awaited him only a few steps away. His body trembled as he weighed up whether Mitch would allow him to keep the bottle after putting him through a load of taunting.

The livery man's silent question was never answered. Another shot fired, the whiskey bottle exploded, and a bullet implanted itself into a side wall of the Mule Kick.

Colt immediately swung his arm to aim his .45 directly at Mitch. 'Holster the gun. Now.'

Mitch looked at the weapon in his hand. 'You think you can take me down before I put a bullet in you?'

'Yes. Holster the gun, right now.'

'This ain't none of your business, stranger.'

'I'm through talking. Holster the gun.'

The barfly once again looked at his gun, then stared at Reverend Colt. Sounds like those of a battle came from outside. Mitch laughed, trying to come across as regarding his opponent to be unworthy of his time. 'Come on, Amos, let's watch the fireworks. Nothin' goin' on in here.' Mitch did what he had been told to do with his gun and left the Mule Kick with his friend.

Skeeter looked at the man who had run off the two barflies, the same man who had destroyed the whiskey bottle. 'Thanks, I guess.'

'Why don't you go outside and enjoy all the fun?' Colt was making a suggestion, not really asking a question. 'Just stay clear of those two troublemakers.'

'Maybe that would be best,' the hostler admitted. 'Might keep my mind off … things.' A strong light flashed across the sky from the fireworks as Skeeter stepped through the batwing doors.

'What would you like?' George asked.

'Huh?' Colt's mind had been far away.

'What can I get you to drink?'

'Oh, ah, nothing. I've sort of lost my thirst.' As Colt stepped onto the boardwalk outside the saloon, the fireworks were making a low rumble. The crowd cheered, but to Colt it sounded like an ominous warning.

After the fireworks, the crowd broke up and headed for a variety of locations. Most party goers drifted toward the saloons, but the town's two restaurants were also doing well. Colt joined the large group of people who gathered behind the *Brother Joseph's Traveling Wonders* box wagon. Like the others, he had been attracted by a singing voice far superior to any of those accompanying the pianos in the saloons.

Mandy Woods was singing from the back of the wagon to a very enthusiastic crowd, who clapped and sang along. With some amusement, Colt noticed that Phineas Wilsey was in the audience. From the enraptured look on Phineas's face, Colt deduced that Mandy's performance would receive a very good review in the town's newspaper.

After Mandy finished with 'Oh Suzanna', her father, who had been standing behind her, stepped forward with a bottle in his hand. Joseph Woods was now wearing a gray suit with a black string tie and white Stetson perched on top of his head. 'Ladies and gentlemen,' he shouted in a loud, pious voice, 'the music will continue in a moment but first, I want to take this occasion to bring you a few words about a magnificent brew.'

'A few words!' Mandy loudly strummed her guitar and looked shocked. 'This guy talks more than an old man bragging about the time he captured one hundred bandits single-handed.'

Good-natured laughter skittered across the crowd. Joseph Woods pretended to look irritated and then continued,

'Brother Joe's Miracle Elixir will soothe your nerves and give you a relaxed temperament.'

'Maybe you should drink some of that stuff.' Mandy's eyes darted between her father and the audience. 'Your nerves weren't very calm this afternoon when I asked if I could buy a new bonnet.'

Joseph Woods looked increasingly irritated as the audience's laughter picked up. 'Why, Brother Joe's Miracle Elixir will put a new bounce and energy in your step!'

'Are you kidding?!' Mandy shot back. 'The last person who drank a bottle of that stuff couldn't walk straight for a week.'

Colt laughed along with the rest of the crowd. He was enjoying the performance, which was far better than the usual medicine show. Mandy and her father were being honest about the fact that the Miracle Elixir was worthless. Buying the stuff was a way of paying for the entertainment.

Colt watched carefully as a man from the audience put both hands on the back of the wagon and very clumsily lifted himself on board. Was this part of the show? Paul Colten moved in closer to the wagon.

'I'd like to buy a bottle of that miracle stuff.' The newcomer weaved as he got to his feet. The man was clearly drunk. Colt was now standing only a few feet away, near the left side of the wagon.

'Why, of course, sir.' Joseph Woods's voice boomed. 'I'm happy to announce that a bottle of Brother Joe's Miracle Elixir can be yours for only thirty-five cents.'

'But it won't cure a hangover,' Mandy quickly added. The father and daughter team had obviously dealt with situations like this before.

The crowd once again began to laugh. Colt became tense. There was a look of desperation and anguish on the face of the drunk that didn't reflect the giddiness of a celebrator having a good time.

'I wanna buy a miracle for Mr Leonard Caldwell.' The drunk waved an arm over the crowd. His red hair and beard both looked scraggly; he was not a man who paid much heed to his appearance. 'You folks all know what a nice fella Mr Caldwell is. Why, he buys people's property for about half of what it's worth. So kind, so gener . . . gener. . . .'

Colt spotted some strange movement near the front of the wagon. He tilted his head and saw two men hastily talking. One had his back to Colt; the other man boarded *Brother Joseph's Traveling Wonders* and reached for the brake.

Colt yelled at the people on the wagon. 'Off, everyone off!'

Joseph Woods looked at the man who had rescued both his daughter and himself only a few hours ago. The Reverend was serious and that was enough for Joe. He grabbed Mandy's hand. The young woman steadied her guitar with her free arm and father and daughter jumped off the wagon.

'I ain't leavin',' the drunk shouted defiantly at Paul Colten. 'You're workin' for Caldwell, jus' like—'

Colt jumped on to the wagon as it took off and rapidly gained speed. The drunk fell backwards into a sitting position and then began to roll. Colt tried to keep his balance as he stumbled toward the front of the wagon where there was a door that led to the driver's seat. The wagon began to shake and weave. Whoever was driving the contraption knew nothing or cared nothing about driving a wagon.

A collision knocked the gunfighter over and he bounced around the floor in a swarm of crashing bottles. From outside came screams and the panicked neighing of horses. A second collision hurled him against one of the sides and back on to the floor as the wagon came to a stop. A liquid stream ran down Colt's shirt, but it wasn't blood. A broken bottle of Brother Joe's Miracle Elixir had splashed on him.

Paul Colten touched the liquid with an index finger and quickly tasted it. 'Sarsaparilla,' he said to himself in an amused voice. 'Harmless enough, and better than what most snake oil salesmen peddle.'

Colt tossed aside the curtain rod that now lay across his knees and got to his feet slowly, avoiding the broken glass. His head felt sore, but a few quick pats indicated it wasn't bleeding. A moan came from the back of the wagon. The gunman made his way to the drunk, who appeared bruised but not seriously harmed.

'Caldwell did this!' the drunk proclaimed and then continued the babble he had begun a few minutes earlier.

The injured man's complaints were drowned out by a loud shout. 'That's him, the guy who rode the wagon, then jumped when it crashed.'

More shouts and the sounds of scrambling feet came from outside. Apparently, the crowd was closing in on the culprit. Colt once again caressed a sore spot on top of his head. 'Hope they hang him.'

Colt looked back down at the drunk. The man was now quiet and glancing about as if trying to figure out what had happened. 'Take your time getting up. This wagon will be here for a while.'

Colt left his companion and jumped from the back of the wagon. He spotted the crowd nearby.

The gunman did a quick inspection of the wreckage. The wagon had collided twice with the platform that the mayor and Leonard Caldwell had used and was now tilted against it. Someone had turned the horses loose. They appeared OK, if a bit spooked, but at least one of the wagon's wheels looked in serious need of repair.

'You're not a deputy anymore, Ox! I'll handle this!' Sheriff Dixon's voice was angry.

'I'm still a citizen and I am a bona fide witness. I saw Harry Blackburn here climb on that wagon and rile the horses. I know just why he did it, too!'

Again, there were loud shouts from the crowd, all of whom appeared to be backing Ox. Colt hurried over to join the debate.

'Well, Ox, it so happens you weren't the only witness,' Sheriff Dixon said confidently. 'I saw what happened. Harry noticed that the wagon's brake wasn't set. That could be dangerous in a crowded town. Being a good deputy, he climbed up to set it, but something spooked the horses and—'

'You're lying, the brake was set!' Mandy Woods shouted angrily. 'What kind of sheriff are you?' Joseph Woods placed a hand on his daughter's shoulder as the crowd shouted out in her favor.

'Young lady, you sing a pretty song, so you just stick to that and to selling snake oil, and leave the law to me,' Dixon snapped back angrily.

'I'm willing to take Miss Woods's word for that.' Colt stepped through the crowd and faced the sheriff. 'And I think most folks here would, too.'

'Well, well, Reverend Colt. You've already killed one man today. Disappointed that no one got trampled when the wagon went out of control?'

The sheriff was looking increasingly nervous. Colt continued to stare at him. 'I saw someone talking with your deputy before he boarded the wagon. Can't be sure, but from where I was standing, that someone looked a lot like you.'

'That's right interestin', Colt, because there are a lot of men who saw what happened and they will back me.' Dixon gave the people around him a threatening look. 'What about it, Fred, you were right here, you saw it all, didn't you?'

Fred, a thin, unarmed man, looked about nervously. 'Why,

ah, yes, Lou, I saw everything.'

'And my account is the true story, right?'

'Yeah, yeah, Lou, that's right.'

Lou Dixon called on two other men and got the same responses. The people in the crowd who had supported Ox and Mandy Woods when they could remain safely anonymous were now backing away and remaining silent.

Colt glanced behind him and saw the drunk, whom he had left in the wagon, making his way toward the crowd. He had somehow managed to climb out of the wreckage and was walking in a straight manner. Apparently, being in a wagon crash and the scent of sarsaparilla had sobered him up to some degree. As he approached, a woman coming from the other end of town shouted the name 'Tom' and ran toward him.

Tom embraced the woman and together they walked toward the sheriff. They did not receive a pleasant greeting. 'Tom Noonan, you're spending the night in jail for being disorderly and drunk.'

'Please, Sheriff,' the woman pleaded. 'My husband never intended—'

'I think we can show a little compassion here, Sheriff Dixon.' The crowd parted, making a path for him as Leonard Caldwell stepped toward the sheriff and pointed at the accused. 'I'm sure that Tom is sorry for all the trouble he has caused and, after all, this is a night for celebration and good cheer.'

The look on Tom Noonan's face was one of raw hatred. 'I don't want none of your—'

Tom's wife hastily cut in. 'Thank you, Mr Caldwell. We're obliged for your kindness.'

Caldwell waved a hand as if graciously dismissing the lady's gratitude. 'Think nothing of it, Ruth. Just keep an eye on that husband of yours. You know, he can get ornery and out of hand at times.'

There was an element of threat in that statement and both Ruth and Tom Noonan caught it. Colt noted that Ruth Noonan had a great deal in common with Tom. She was an attractive woman but a hard life had not allowed her to spend much time on her appearance. Her hair was reddish brown and the malice in her eyes as she looked at Leonard Caldwell could match that of her husband. She had forced herself to spit out the proper words to Caldwell.

Caldwell looked at Mandy Woods. 'Young lady, this town could sure use a few more songs from you. Let me make a deal with you. You go over there to the boardwalk and do some more singing, and I'll pay to have that wagon of yours fixed!'

The offer seemed to restore the mood of celebration. Mandy sang four songs from the boardwalk, ending, as she had suggested to her father that afternoon, with the lively and spiritual 'Swing Low, Sweet Chariot'. When the music was finished, several people offered Mandy and her father some money for the entertainment. Colt noticed that Joseph Woods looked very uneasy as he took the cash.

'I sure appreciated your fine singin'.' Ox spoke to Mandy as the crowd was breaking up. 'That wagon will take a while to fix. Think maybe ya could sing in church this Sunday? I do the preachin', and to be honest, I ain't much of an attraction.'

'Oh, does Grayson have a church?'

'Nah, hope to some day, but meanwhiles we meet every Sunday in the Mule Kick Saloon. The Mule Kick don't sell whiskey on Sunday until 1 p.m., out of respect for the Sabbath. Course, most of our customers get pretty drunk on Saturday night, anyways, so they mostly sleep in till noon.'

'I'd like to do it … sing in church, I mean.'

Ox shouted to the dispersing crowd, which was now scattered all over the town's main street. 'Hear that, folks? Miss Mandy Woods will be singin' at the Mule Kick this Sunday morning.

Only during church time; she ain't singin' once they start to serve whiskey. So be there at ten in the mornin'!'

Several shouts of approval came from different sections of the street. Ox looked pleased. 'In the Good Book, this is called proclaimin' the good news.'

Among the small group of people still gathered around Mandy and her father stood Ruth and Tom Noonan. Ruth spoke while her husband looked on. 'Tom and me feel awful about what has happened to you folks. Do you two sleep in the wagon most nights?'

Joseph Woods nodded his head. 'Some nights we camp out. Reckon that's what—'

'You're welcome to stay with us until the wagon gets fixed,' Tom interrupted. He spoke in an embarrassed tone. 'Please, this is all my fault. I want to make it up to you.'

'We'd be happy to accept your generosity,' Joseph said, impressed by the intensity of Tom's remorse.

Skeeter, who was also standing nearby, abruptly spoke up. 'I know all 'bout gettin' a busted wagon to move. We'll put it behind the livery. Lots of room there.' Skeeter looked at Colt as if seeking assurance that his helpfulness compensated for his earlier behavior at the Mule Kick. Receiving a positive nod from the former clergyman, Skeeter hurried off to get the move organized.

'I also have an offer!' Up to this point, no one had been paying much attention to Phineas Wilsey. 'The *Grayson Herald* is a prospering enterprise, and I am in need of assistants. I would like to hire both of you, starting first thing tomorrow morning!'

Phineas hoped that he sounded convincing. The *Grayson Herald* had benefited from extra advertising brought on by the town's tenth anniversary celebration, but he could only pay Joseph and Mandy Woods for a day or two of work. He didn't exactly understand his own bravado, but he desperately wanted to impress Mandy Woods.

'Hire us to do what, Mr ah …?' Joe Woods began to fumble for the name.

'Wilsey, Phineas Wilsey. Remember I was in the sheriff's office?'

'I remember.'

The newspaper man detected that his offer was being met with more than just a trace of skepticism. He put more force in his voice. 'I could show you how to operate the press, Mr Woods. For a man of your strength and intelligence it would be an easy task.' Phineas saw immediately that his compliment had not impressed Joseph Woods. He looked at Mandy. 'And Miss Woods, I am certain that a woman with your creative talents would make an excellent proofreader and reporter.'

A gleam came into the young woman's eyes. She turned to her father. 'Dad, we are going to be here for a while, it wouldn't hurt to—'

'Mandy, we'll probably be pulling out in a few days.'

'And meanwhile, we can help Mr Wilsey.'

Colt smiled inwardly. Joseph Woods's distrust of Phineas was strong, but he couldn't say no to his daughter. After more gentle pleading from Mandy, Joseph reluctantly agreed to the newspaper man's 'generous offer' and shook his hand.

'I'll help you get your horses over to the livery,' Phineas proclaimed. 'You can rent saddles there, if your horses are—'

'I know how the livery operates, Mr Wilsey!' The irritation in Joseph Woods's voice was apparent as he walked toward his horses and busted wagon. 'And, yes, every one of our horses can take a saddle very well, thank you!'

Colt noted that Mandy, Ruth and Tom Noonan all looked a tad uneasy as they walked behind Joe and Phineas, but the newspaper man didn't seem at all bothered by Joseph's sarcasm. The gunfighter laughed quietly as he wondered if Phineas had been the target of so much sarcasm that he could no longer recognize it.

His musings were short-lived. 'You're Reverend Colt? The gunfighter that once was a preacher?'

'That's me. And from what I gather you're Ox and you used to be a deputy sheriff here in Grayson.'

' "Use ta be" is the part Sheriff Dixon likes to put the most emphasis on.'

'What exactly happened with your old job, Ox?' Both men paused in the street, near the boardwalk, as the others moved on toward the broken wagon and the horses. 'Did the sheriff you were serving with lose an election?'

'Never got the chance; he was murdered. They tried to make it look like a accident – that he shot himself while cleanin' a gun. They made it a big joke. A lawman who couldn't even clean his own gun. Well, I knew Russ Jones, and nothin' like that happened. A couple o' barflies got paid to claim they witnessed the whole thing. A good man's reputation was ruined by two snakes that'd say anythin' for a free drink.'

Colt took a long breath and looked around him. The hour was getting later. Families were leaving for home. Soon the night would belong to the revelers and gamblers: men trying to find a touch of heaven in a bottle, the cards or the false smile of a lady who would whisper familiar lies for the right price.

'How did Lou Dixon get the job as sheriff?' Colt asked.

'After Russ was killed, I became actin' sheriff for about two weeks. The mayor called a special election for sheriff. Lou Dixon was the only man runnin'. I tried to put my name in, but they said there was somethin' wrong about the papers I filled out. Not too many folks bothered to vote. But then, one vote woulda' done it for Lou Dixon.'

'From what I can tell, Leonard Caldwell is the man who runs just about everything in this town. Was he responsible for Russ

Jones's death?'

Ox nodded his head vigorously. 'Yeah. I know that Caldwell jasper through and through. That's sorta why I'm talkin' to ya.'

'What do you mean?'

'Leonard Caldwell plans to kill another man tonight. Will ya help me stop it?'

CHAPTER FIVE

Ruth Noonan closed the bedroom door behind her and smiled at the two guests who sat at the dining table. 'Tom is sleeping now. He'll have a headache in the morning, but he's fine.' The woman looked at the floor as she approached the table. 'Please believe me, Tom doesn't drink much.'

Joseph Woods sipped the coffee Ruth had prepared and tried to think of the right thing to say. For some reason, the pleasant, well-kept home made him nervous. 'I'm sure that is true, Mrs Noonan. There is a lot of pressure that comes from running a horse ranch.'

'The horses aren't the problem. Leonard Caldwell is the one causing the trouble.' Ruth spoke as she sat at the table.

Mandy Woods's fingers drummed excitedly on her coffee cup. She had heard stories about Caldwell during their previous visits to Grayson. Now, here was a chance to really get the goods on the brute. What a way to start her career as a journalist.

'How has Caldwell been causing you trouble, Mrs Noonan?' Her first question as a reporter; not bad for a start, the young woman thought to herself.

'Leonard Caldwell wants this land,' Ruth replied. 'You'd think he'd be happy with all he has, but no. About four months ago, he offered to buy us out for less than half of what this spread is worth. We turned him down. A few weeks later, horses were stampeded from our corral in the middle of the night. We weren't able to fulfill a contract we had with the army.'

'Has Caldwell directly threatened you?' Mandy continued the interview.

'He talked about what a dangerous place the West can be. A few months before, he had offered to buy out the Bower family. They said no and, less than a week later, their spread burned down. The entire family, five people, died in the flames.' Ruth sighed, glanced down at the table and then looked back at her guest. 'Ox claims that every one of those bodies had bullets in them. But they were buried that day. Sheriff Dixon never investigated.'

Mandy Woods felt a sudden sense of shame over her playful attitude. This wasn't a game. This was a case of real people facing a life-or-death situation.

Colt and Ox tied their horses near the top of a large hill, which formed a horseshoe around the Noonans' ranch house. 'Enough trees here to provide cover,' Ox whispered. 'In case Caldwell's men come from this direction, they probably won't spot 'em.'

'But you think they'll attack from the opposite side?' Colt also spoke in a whisper.

'Yeah, easier to get to the corral. They'll want to loose the horses. Make it look like stealin' nags was the big idea, like killin' just naturally followed.'

Ox led Colt down the hill to a boulder, which gave them good cover as well as a clear view of the ranch house and the corral, which stood about fifteen yards to the far side of it. Colt carried his Winchester while Ox toted a Henry. 'They won't show for a few hours yet,' Ox said confidently, 'But I'm a cautious man by nature.'

Both men were quiet for a while, carefully looking over the surrounding area. They spotted nothing unusual and heard only the sounds of crickets, rustling leaves, small varmints, and the casual neighing of the horses in the corral.

'You're sure something is going to happen here tonight, Ox?'

'Yep, I know Leonard Caldwell real well. He won't tolerate a man standing up in front of a crowd speakin' against him.'

'Even if the man is drunk?' Colt smiled at his own question.

'Yep. Those kinds of details don't interest Caldwell much. All that nice talk he made tonight about showin' compassion to poor Tom Noonan, he thinks that's enough for folks not to suspect him of doin' somethin' bad to Tom. Caldwell's thinkin' ain't subtle.'

'What's Caldwell after?'

'He wants the biggest spread in Texas and won't be happy till he has it. He will get rid of anyone who stands in the way of those plans. Known a few men like that in my day. Caldwell is a mite different, though.'

'How's that, Ox?'

'Caldwell wants people to like him. As long as he's gettin' his own way, he can be nice to folks. He paid for those fireworks you saw tonight.'

'Does it work? I mean, do people like him?'

'Nah, but they pretend they do. They know what happens to people who go up against Leonard Caldwell.'

'They end up dead.'

'Yep. That tends to encourage folks to be real careful about their manners when they're around Leonard.'

The Noonans' house went dark. That signaled Ox and Colt to limit their conversations. For a few hours, the men took turns sleeping. Colt had been dozing for about twenty minutes when he felt Ox's hand slap his shoulder.

As the gunman moved into a crouch behind the boulder, Ox pointed upward toward the opposite side of the hill. A light blinked as it moved between the trees.

'Perfect timing.' Ox's whisper was tinged with bitterness. 'Everyone inside is probably asleep. I bet this is just what they did to the Bowers when they killed them all, kids included.'

The light moved down the hill cautiously like a monstrous firefly stalking its prey. Not until he reached the bottom of the hill and rode slowly away from the trees could the outline of the horseman carrying the lantern be seen. He rode directly toward the house, stopping about ten yards away from the door. Two other riders pulled up to the left and right of him as they drew rifles from the boots of their saddles.

Another pair of thugs stopped near the corral. One of them dismounted and approached the house, carrying a torch. He stopped and flamed a matchstick with his thumbnail.

'You may think me crazy, Reverend, but I'm still a lawdog at heart.' Ox bolted up, his large figure looming over the boulder. 'You men freeze right where ya are!'

No one obeyed the order; that didn't surprise the ex-lawman, who was quick with the Henry. His first shot brought down the only outlaw who hadn't gone for his gun. The man who had been holding the torch stumbled backwards, then hit the ground. The torch spiraled harmlessly toward the corral. The burning match went out as it landed on the red stain that was quickly spreading across the would-be arsonist's chest.

Colt fired his first shot into one of the horsemen near the door of the house holding a rifle. As the rifle fell and its owner fell on it, the rider holding the lantern fired his pistol toward the boulder. That would be the final time he threatened anyone. Colt's next shot slammed him off his horse. The lantern landed on its side, still casting out some light while leaking kerosene on to the ground.

Joseph Woods appeared at the door of the house and squeezed off a shot from his Peacemaker at the remaining horseman near the house. The outlaw was already riding off, and the shot missed. As the retreating horseman passed the corral, his one remaining colleague opened the corral gate and fired into the air, stampeding the horses.

Two more shots spurted red from Joseph's pistol but the escaping outlaws were now barely in sight. Colt and Ox began to scramble downwards toward the cabin. Mandy Woods ran out of the house with Ruth and Tom immediately behind her. The young woman spotted the flickering light on the ground, ran to the lantern and picked it up. With her free hand she scooped up some dirt and scattered it over the kerosene-soaked ground.

'Is everyone all right?' Colt shouted as he and Ox ran toward the house.

For a moment, no one on the porch spoke, as if they were unsure of who was qualified to speak for the group. Mandy broke the silence as she stepped back on to the porch and placed the lantern down. 'I guess so, everyone looks OK to me. We've missed out on a few hours of sleep, but otherwise we're fine.'

There was a moment of cathartic laughter from both the Noonans and the Woods, a way of expressing relief and gratitude that they were still alive and unharmed, despite the fact that a gang of killers had just come after them. Ox began a check on the three outlaws, who were now scattered about the front of the Noonan house. Only one of them was still alive, the man who had been carrying the lantern.

'Hello, Stacy.' Ox crouched over the outlaw writhing in pain on the ground. 'Not surprised to see ya here. You never seemed to be much of a ranch-hand. Caldwell paid ya as a hired gun, didn't he?'

'Get me . . . doctor. . . .'

'Too late for that!' Ox snapped as Colt quietly approached and stood behind him. 'In a few minutes you'll be standin' before your Maker. The conversation will be right unpleasant. I'm givin' ya a chance to maybe make it a little better. Just maybe. Can't promise nothin'.'

'Whaddya mean?'

'I'm askin' some questions and you're gonna tell the truth. Won't hurt ya none. You'll be dead soon. Caldwell can't get to ya.'

'But he can get to you, Ox,' the wounded man replied. 'Caldwell hates you.'

'Why?'

' 'Cause you're crazy loco 'bout the law. The boss knew he'd have a time running the other ranchers off with you and Russ Jones wearing tin stars.'

'Did you kill Russ?'

'Yeah, ambushed. . . .' Stacy's eyes indicated that a new wave of pain was hitting him. 'Can't you get doctor. . . ?'

'No. You were in on the killing of the Bower family, too. Same plan ya used here.'

'Yeah. How'd you know 'bout what we done?'

'Heard ya and some other hardcases makin' jokes about Dave Bower while I was tendin' bar in the Mule Kick one night. At first, I thought it was just talk. I put things together too late. When I got to the Bowers' place there was only ashes and dead bodies.'

Stacy's voice became faint. 'We burned the house, then shot them as they ran out. . . .' The outlaw's body began to twist as if he were having a violent seizure.

'Stacy, you're as no good as they come. But there is still hope for ya. Ask for forgiveness, say you're sorry.'

'I'm sorry, all right. Sorry you weren't visitin' the Bowers that night, Ox. Sorry you weren't burned. . . .' The killer gave a loud scream of pain, then his body went limp.

Ox shook his head as he stood up. He took a slow look all around, taking in the dead bodies of the three outlaws. 'Told ya I was a lawdog at heart. Guess I'm a better lawdog than a preacher.'

Colt briefly placed a hand on Ox's shoulder but said nothing.

The two men walked back to the porch where the mood of giddy relief was now turning somber. Tom Noonan stared at the empty corral. 'Why'd they have to run the horses off?'

'Probably hoping to create a distraction,' Joseph answered. 'And it makes it a lot harder to track 'em. Especially since we'll have to wait till sunup, anyhow.'

'Don't have to track 'em.' Tom panted out angry breaths as he spoke. 'They're riding right to Caldwell's spread.'

Ox spoke quietly, trying to calm the rancher. 'Yeah, but I suspect none of us saw their faces good.' He quickly looked at his companions and received nods indicating that he had gotten it right. 'Caldwell will claim he just fired the three jaspers we got here. None of the men who are working for him now had anything to do with it. With Lou Dixon as sheriff, that's all the story he needs.'

'The horses are gone.' Tom's voice was now almost a sob. 'I'm supposed to have horses for the army by next week. This will be the second time straight I didn't make a contract.'

'I'll help you round them up,' Joseph offered. 'I reckon most of them didn't go too far. If you can put up with Mandy and me for a few more days, we should be able to get that corral full.'

Tom looked dubious. 'Won't be easy.'

Mandy gave the rancher a lopsided grin. 'Can't be any tougher than selling snake oil.'

That line brought on smiles all around, even from Tom. Ruth Noonan tried to buttress the good mood. 'None of us is

46

likely to get any more sleep tonight. You fellas got some plant-ing to do; Mandy and me will rustle us up some breakfast.'

As he began to dig a grave, Colt's mind was fixed on Leonard Caldwell. Stopping the man from his killing spree had not been the reason he came to Grayson, Texas. But, it did sort of fit in. . . .

Mandy's mind was also churning as she worked beside Ruth. With her father helping Tom, she would be starting her first day as a journalist alone with her new boss, Phineas Wilsey. That thought made her nervous but, she had to admit, it also excited her. She couldn't rid herself of the feeling that the next few days were going to be very important.

CHAPTER SIX

'That all, Mr Caldwell?'

Leonard Caldwell sipped his newly poured coffee. 'Excellent! Thank you, Donny, I don't need anything else.'

The Asian man graciously but quickly disappeared into the kitchen. He knew his boss always wanted to have breakfast by himself in the dining room.

Caldwell could no longer remember Donny's real name. But he remembered the day three years ago when he had found Donny close to death inside a ripped tent. Donny had been working as a cook for the railroad as it laid track. He had become seriously ill while the outfit was in Grayson, and the people in charge would no longer have anything to do with him. When they abandoned the camp, they abandoned Donny.

The ranch owner cut into his steak and reflected on the fact that he had paid for a doctor to care for Donny and then had given him a job when the young man recovered. Hardly anyone in town knew about it until that newspaper fellow from the East arrived in Grayson. The first edition of the paper had contained the story about Leonard Caldwell, the Good Samaritan.

Caldwell sampled his eggs. They were fried just the way he liked them. Supporting Grayson's first newspaper and encouraging the merchants to advertise in it had been a wise move.

Now, whenever Donny went into town for supplies, people were reminded of what a generous man they had in their community.

And, he would continue to need the paper. There were people who opposed him – that would always be the case. Stephen Hayworth, for one. Hayworth had hired Ox as a jack of all trades just to taunt him, but Hayworth's victory was hollow. Ox was no real threat to him now that he had complete control over the man who was wearing the sheriff's badge.

Caldwell sat back feeling contented. He smiled at the portrait which faced him from the dining room's west wall. The painting had been done twelve years before and showed a younger Caldwell with his wife and 5-year-old daughter. Life had been so wonderful then, so uncomplicated. A year later, the only two people he really loved were gone, both stolen from him by the same terrible disease. He had made them a solemn promise: 'Someday the Bar C will be the biggest spread in Texas.' Keeping that promise was the one thing in life that he truly cared about.

'For you,' he whispered aloud to the portrait as there was a knock at the front door. Donny hurried through the dining room and returned a few moments later.

'Two men, Phil and Dutcher, say must see you right away.' Donny didn't ask his boss if he should show them in. Leonard Caldwell never tolerated company in the dining room during breakfast.

'Thank you,' Caldwell sighed, and rose from the table. The one part of the day that he cherished had just been taken from him.

As he marched into the living room, his stomach tightened. He didn't like the chagrinned looks on the faces of his hired guns.

'Yes?' The rancher's voice was harsh.

Dutcher spoke first. 'Things didn't go well at the Noonan

place, boss. They sorta surprised us.'

'What do you mean?'

'They was waitin' for us,' Phil said.

Leonard Caldwell's anger was building as he noted the blank looks in the eyes of the two hired guns. He was paying them good money; was it too much to ask for good work?

'Tell me what happened!'

'Well, we got set up just like with the Bower place,' Phil said.

'And then what?'

'Suddenly Ox pops up out of nowhere.' Dutcher's words were high-pitched and shrill. 'He starts to shootin' at us.'

'One man took on five of you!'

'No.' Phil spoke up quickly, this was a matter of pride. 'He had help; that guy who jumped on the wagon last night, the gunfighter, Reverend Colt.'

Caldwell's voice suddenly became low and thoughtful. 'I saw him in town last night. Know him by reputation, but I thought he was just passing through.'

'I don't think so, boss.' Phil was grateful for the diversion from talking about the disastrous failure at the Noonan place. 'Seems like he's gonna be in town for a while.'

'We need to find out why he's here.' Caldwell was now talking mainly to himself. 'Or maybe we don't. The important thing is that he never causes us any more trouble. If he does, we kill him.'

CHAPTER SEVEN

Phineas Wilsey tried to look busy as he sat at his desk, occasionally eyeing Mandy Woods, who sat at a much smaller desk, reading over articles he had asked her to proofread. Their day together had begun awkwardly. Mandy had rushed into the office about fifteen minutes earlier, talking about a shooting at the Noonan Ranch.

'I was there and saw it all … well, I saw most of it and got details from Ox and Reverend Colt. I'll write the story up right now. Mr Noonan has even given me permission to quote him as saying that Leonard Caldwell is behind it all!'

'Ah.' Phineas fumbled about in his mind for a diversion. 'Where is your father, Miss Woods?'

'He couldn't come. . . .' She hastily explained that Joe would be helping Tom Noonan round up enough horses to fulfill his contract with the army.

'That's wonderful!' Phineas exclaimed. 'I mean, it's wonderful that your father is able to help Tom Noonan in his hour of need.'

'Yes.' There was a questioning note in Mandy's voice. 'Shouldn't I get started on that article now?'

'Well, first, I'd like you to proof a few articles I have already written.' He laughed and shook his head, feigning humility.

'They are just trifles, but—'

'Can't the trifles wait? This is an important story!'

'Please, Miss Woods. After all, you are here to learn how to be a journalist. I can't help you if you won't follow my instructions.'

As Phineas now watched his new protégé he realized he had been far too bossy. Mandy had obeyed his instructions, but her face appeared gloomy as she read the articles in front of her. Well, that would soon change! She would soon be reading the article that Phineas had written about her performance the previous evening.

Following the fireworks, the citizens of Grayson were treated to the angelic voice of Miss Mandy Woods, who performed a variety of songs and then displayed a marvelous comedic ability in a routine she flawlessly performed with her father, Joseph.

Phineas anxiously anticipated the moment when the young lady would read his review. She would probably smile at him shyly and say something like, 'Mr Wilsey, you are much too kind.'

He would smile back confidently and reply, 'Miss Woods, you deserve every word of praise that I wrote. And, please, call me New York, everybody does.'

No, that wouldn't work. To begin with, no one called him New York, despite his recent prodding of the local townsfolk in that direction. It didn't seem fair. They called the proprietor of Benson's Mercantile Utah, despite the fact that he hadn't lived in Utah since he was a boy, why—

'This is awful!' Mandy slapped a hand on her desk and stood up as if disconnecting from the written words in front of her.

'What do you mean?' Phineas stood up and did a hasty walk to his new assistant.

'This article of yours, it's awful.' She pointed at the papers on her desk. 'OK, so Leonard Caldwell paid for the fireworks, but you make the guy sound like Santa Claus.'

'Well—'

She picked up one of the papers and began to read. '*Mr Caldwell's delightful comment that when the town was incorporated, he still had a full head of hair had the entire crowd bent over in laughter.* That's a lie. Nobody laughed.'

'Some people did.'

'And that stuff about a drunken lout interrupting the show.'

'Tom Noonan was drunk when he—'

'Did you ever think of asking Tom why he got drunk, Mr Wilsey? I did, and those reasons should be in the newspaper.'

'Look—'

'Are you a real newspaper man or are you just another lapdog for Leonard Caldwell?'

Phineas didn't know how to answer that question, even to himself. He was spared the effort. The door to the newspaper office opened and three men entered: Reverend Colt, Ox, and a man of forty-some years with iron-gray hair and the bearing of a former military man.

'Ah, good morning.' Phineas sensed that something was about to be dumped on him. He had no idea what.

'Mornin', Phineas, Miss Woods.' Ox nodded at Mandy, then faced the newspaper editor. 'We need some help, Phineas, and you are just the man for the job.'

Phineas Wilsey was feeling increasingly nervous. Two of the three men in front of him were hated by Leonard Caldwell and Phineas was positive that the rancher would have little regard for the Reverend. Without Caldwell's support, there would be no *Grayson Herald.* Wilsey wanted the men out of his office. Fast.

The man with the iron-gray hair spoke. 'Mr Wilsey, before we begin, I owe you an apology.'

The editor smiled and shrugged his shoulders. 'Why is that, Mr Hayworth?'

'I haven't advertised in the *Herald* because I thought the paper was nothing more than a tool for Leonard Caldwell to tighten his grip on this town.' Stephen Hayworth nodded to the man on his immediate left. 'But Ox is the most trustworthy man I know and he told me about why you lost your job in New York.'

'I told him all 'bout your journalistic integrity,' Ox proclaimed enthusiastically. 'How you wrote the truth even though it angered your boss and got ya tossed into the street.'

Mandy Woods turned to Phineas with something in her eyes that he never wanted to see disappear. 'I didn't know about this, Mr Wilsey.' Her voice sounded just as it had in his daydream.

'Well, there was hardly any need to tell you about it.' Phineas quickly decided that a low-key, modest approach would work best here. He paused, allowing the young woman time to ask him to tell her the story of his journalistic integrity.

She never got the chance. Colt spoke first. 'We're going to be needing that courage right here in Grayson, Mr Wilsey.'

Phineas's nervousness returned. 'I don't understand.'

Colt began to pace about the office as he spoke. 'Last night, I caught the mood of that crowd after the wagon was wrecked. They wanted to defy Leonard Caldwell but were afraid. They need leadership and direction, and tomorrow they are going to get it.'

'What do you mean?' Mandy asked.

'Your singing is quite an attraction, Miss Woods. I'm sure there's going to be a large crowd at the Mule Kick tomorrow morning for the church service.' Colt certainly understood that Mandy's singing was not the only attraction for the town's men, but remained silent on that matter. 'After you have gotten everyone in a good mood, Ox is going to tell them that if they stand for what is right and defy Caldwell, they won't be standing alone.'

'You mean, God will be with them,' Mandy said.

Colt seemed embarrassed by the statement. 'Yes, yes, of course. But it goes beyond that. Ox will promise them protection from Leonard Caldwell. Ox is going to form a private army, of sorts.'

'That's what I'm gonna preach about, all right.' Ox blurted out his words enthusiastically, then paused. 'And I'm gonna keep preachin' that till Caldwell is in jail.'

'All this sounds good but, well, I've sung in churches before.' Mandy shook her head. 'People say they are going to do all sorts of wonderful things on Sunday morning, but they forget about it by Monday.'

'Sermons alone won't do it,' Colt agreed. He turned his gaze to Phineas. 'That's where you come in.'

Phineas laughed nervously. 'What can I do?'

'As I understand it, the paper comes out three times a week: Tuesday, Thursday and Saturday.'

The newspaper man nodded his head at Colt's statement.

'The Tuesday edition of the *Grayson Herald* will contain a front-page account of Ox's sermon.' Colt once again paced about the office. 'On Thursday, you can run a story on how different people have reacted to the sermon. Saturday's paper can contain some hints as to what Ox will preach the next day. Follow this pattern for a few weeks. That will get people talking openly about Caldwell's reign of terror and let them know they are not alone in wanting to bring an end to his tyranny in this town.'

'I'd love to do that,' Phineas stammered. 'But—'

'But what?' Mandy almost shouted. 'It's a great idea!'

'Running a newspaper costs money.' Phineas lowered his voice, trying to sound like a pragmatic businessman. 'If I start running articles critical of Leonard Caldwell, all of the merchants will pull their advertising.'

'I've thought of that.' Stephen Hayworth smiled at Phineas. 'Beginning this Tuesday, I will advertise in every edition of the *Herald*. I'll promote my saloons, the livery, and even run an ad on Saturday urging folks to attend the Sunday service at the Mule Kick.'

'That should be enough to keep you going until we knock Humpty Dumpty off his wall.' Colt eyed Phineas carefully.

He wasn't the only one. Phineas saw the look that Mandy gave him. The adoration had been replaced with a questioning appraisal. The young man could hardly believe his own voice as he spoke out. 'I will do everything I can to rid this town of such a horrible plague. The duty of a journalist is to protect the citizenry by proclaiming the truth!'

Cheers followed Phineas's bold pronouncement. The giddiness was quickly followed by a sober discussion of what lay ahead. Only Colt noticed that the newspaper editor kept his hands in his pockets much of the time. Colt also knew why: Phineas's hands were shaking.

As he walked from the newspaper office to the hotel, Colt could hear light footsteps behind him. He turned and faced Mandy Woods just as she called out his name.

'Sorry to be a bother, Reverend.'

She was making him edgy, but Colt tried not to show it. 'Not at all, Miss Woods.'

'I won't take much of your time. I can't. I need to get back to the newspaper office.'

'The *Grayson Herald* is going to be taking up a lot of your time for a spell.' He hoped she had questions about the newspaper or the next morning's service at the Mule Kick.

Those hopes were quickly dashed. 'Reverend Colt, do you intend to settle down in Grayson?'

'No, Miss Woods, I don't.'

'Then, why are you doing so much to help this town? And why did you come here in the first place?'

Colt's laugh came out sounding a bit nervous. 'You are a very inquisitive young lady, Miss Woods. You'll make an excellent reporter.'

'I hope most people I interview aren't as good at avoiding questions as you are, Reverend Colt.'

Colt's only response was to broaden his smile. When Mandy spoke again, her voice was soft and sympathetic. 'I think there is quite a story that goes with you, Reverend Colt. Maybe I'll never write it. Maybe no one will. People say you were once a preacher and now you are no more than a gun for hire. My father and I know better. You've gone out of your way to protect us, more than once.'

Colt looked toward the sky. For a moment he wanted to tell this young woman everything. But Mandy Woods was a very special young lady, only just finding her direction in life. She didn't need his burdens. 'I'm very glad that you and your father think well of me.'

'I also can see that you are a very private man, Reverend Colt. So, I'll respect your privacy.' She paused, then offered him a sly smile. 'For the time being. I am now a journalist, you know.'

They both laughed and then parted. Mandy walked briskly back to the newspaper office. As he once again headed for the hotel, Colt noticed that, like Phineas Wilsey, his hands were shaking.

CHAPTER EIGHT

Colt leaned back from the desk and looked at his notes. He carefully reread the open Bible in front of him to make sure he had quoted the verses correctly. The former clergyman was glad he would only have to help Ox with one of his sermons.

'Ain't never preached anything like this before, and in front of a big crowd,' Ox had told him. 'Any help ya might be with my sermon tomorrow would be appreciated. After that, I'll have the hang of it.'

Colt laughed quietly. He was sure Ox would bring his unique personality to anything someone else had written.

The gunman glanced out of the hotel room window, then stared at the wall in front of him. Ox's idealism and the idealism of Mandy Woods and Stephen Hayworth impressed him greatly. Phineas Wilsey was a little harder to peg. At the very least, Wilsey was making a good effort at achieving idealistic goals. He recalled the look on Phineas's face when Mandy Woods was singing. OK, so Phineas's good deeds were prompted by his desire to please a young lady. Men have been motivated by far worse, Colt thought.

Colt continued to stare at the wall in front of him as he thought back on the idealism of his own youth. His reflections brought him no comfort.

*

He had been a theology student studying at a seminary in Boston when he met Christina. She was the daughter of one of his professors, Dr Hiram Bolger. Dr Bolger had an interest in the West, an interest which had been greatly inflamed by his fondness for dime novels.

Paul Colten's longing to head West was inspired by a desire to help bring faith and stability to the folks who were settling that vast part of the country. 'There are new towns springing up everywhere, Christina!' He spoke as they sat together on the porch of the Bolger home. 'Most of those towns have no church. They need us!'

His eyes shifted from the sky to his fiancée. 'Oh brother! We're not even married yet and I'm trying to convince you to leave your family and the life you have always led.'

Christina smiled and cupped her hands over his. 'You are being called to the West, Paul, and I am being called to be your wife.'

Their calling had started well. They were married two weeks after Paul graduated, and headed West one month later. The population of Sterling, Arizona welcomed them with enthusiasm. Paul Colten began to hold services every Sunday morning under a large sycamore tree. Within a year, a new church had been built.

Paul became a civic as well as a spiritual leader of the town, so he was not surprised when Sheriff Reynolds asked him to stop by his office. Reynolds was a church deacon and his wife played the piano on Sunday mornings, but Sam Reynolds liked to keep his responsibilities separated and Paul figured this matter did not concern the church.

'Thanks fer droppin' by, Paul.' Sam Reynolds smiled at his visitor, who sat on a wooden chair that appeared newer than the battered desk the lawman sat behind. The sheriff was an older man with a rough complexion and a mustache that was mostly gray, but there was no extra weight on his large, muscular build. 'I got me a problem that may be more up your alley. Ever hear of Zack Hogan?'

Paul's eyes widened. 'Who hasn't heard of him? Zack Hogan is one of the fastest guns in the West.'

Sam smiled and nodded his head. 'Yeah, and he is also a home-town boy. He'll be here sometime in the next few days.'

'Are you expecting trouble?'

'Not from Zack,' the lawman shot back. 'He's coming to visit his sister. Gunmen need to take a little time off to relax, just like the rest of us.'

'Guess so. Then what's the problem?'

Sam again replied quickly. 'I know you've heard of Jerry Blaine.'

'Oh yes.' Paul sighed and ran a hand through his hair. 'That kid has made his mother's life a trip through Hades. I keep telling Esther to stop paying for all the damage her son does – make him take his own medicine. Yes, it's a shame his father died when he was young. But Jerry needs to grow up, he's seventeen now and—'

'He's eighteen,' the sheriff interrupted. 'Without much hope of becoming nineteen.'

'What do you mean?'

'Jerry has got the notion he's a gunfighter.' The sheriff drummed his fingers on his desk for a moment, then continued. 'He plans to call Zack Hogan out. Jerry is fast with a gun, but he can't match Hogan.'

'Will Zack Hogan kill him?'

'He'll try not to.' Sam spoke in a matter-of-fact voice. 'But if the kid keeps shoutin' out that Zack is afraid to fight him, well, a gunfighter can't walk away from that.'

Neither man said anything for what seemed a long while. When Paul spoke it was in a whisper. 'What can I do, Sam?'

'Talk to the boy, please. I tried, but nothin' came of it. Maybe you can do better.' The sheriff's voice was vehement. Colten remembered being told that Sam Reynolds had been a close friend of Jerry's father.

'I've talked to Jerry about changing his ways. He won't listen.'

'Keep at it, Paul! The kid's life is at stake!'

A confused and troubled Paul Colten left the sheriff's office and went home to discuss Jerry Blaine with his wife. 'Not one thing I've said has had any effect on Blaine. How can I save his life now?'

'You can't do it alone, Paul,' Christina replied softly. 'I will help you, but first we need to go to the Lord in prayer.'

The couple prayed together and then discussed a course of action. That night, Paul Colten went looking for Jerry Blaine. He knew where to start: the town's most disreputable saloon. As he approached the Happy Times, he heard the shout of a familiar voice followed by gunfire.

Colten ran into the saloon. Jerry Blaine was standing beside the bar with his gun drawn. He had just fired into a wall. 'No man can match that draw,' the kid shouted. 'Not even Zack Hogan. Yeah, they'll be buryin' old Zack sometime soon.'

The denizens of the saloon looked edgy, expecting the kid to shout out a challenge to any man in the place to go against him. The pastor's entrance only upped the tension. Colten could sense eyes following him as he approached the bar.

'Well, well, Reverend, out saving souls?' Jerry Blaine was a tall, well-built kid with a wide mouth that always seemed to be in a sneer.

'Saving your soul could be a full-time job, Jerry.' Light laughter scattered across the saloon as Paul leaned against the bar and with one finger tilted his hat back a few inches on his head. He hoped the casual charade was working.

'You're not wearing a gun, preacher man. Guess they don't teach gunfightin' at that school you went to in the East.'

'Guess not.'

'Well, I'll give you a lesson right now!' He twirled his gun and slammed it into his holster. 'I'm gonna draw and shoot that hat off your head before you have a chance to blink.'

Paul charged the young man, who was stunned by the move and the pastor's speed. Jerry's gun was only halfway out of the holster when Colten smashed a fist under the kid's left ear. Jerry Blaine and his gun hit the floor at about the same time.

Paul picked up the gun, emptied the bullets on to the floor and looked down at the kid, who was struggling to maintain consciousness. 'No, you can't take courses in gunfighting back East, but they do teach boxing.'

Loud laughter exploded in the saloon as Colten stuck the empty pistol in his belt. Paul grabbed the collar of the kid's shirt and dragged him out of the Happy Times, a move intended to humiliate Blaine.

Outside of the saloon, the pastor slammed Blaine against the wall beside the batwing doors and spoke to him in a threatening voice. 'Jerry, there are a lot of people in this town who have been trying to help you and now you are going to pay them back by helping yourself.'

'Whaddya mean?'

'You are going to live with Christina and me for a while. You're going to learn to read, and memorize Scripture verses. The roof of the church needs fixing up and you are going to spend your days working on that.'

'You . . . you would let me live in your home?'

'That's the way it is going to be.'

'What does your wife think about all this?'

'She thinks you are a man in need of saving.'

Jerry Blaine looked down at the boardwalk. 'You have a fine woman, preacher.'

'Yes.'

'Every man should have a woman like Christina Colten.'

'It is all about the kind of life you choose to live, Jerry. That's one of the things we are going to talk about.'

The next day went well. Paul and Jerry did repair work on the church's roof and that night Christina gave the young man his first reading lesson. Before they retired, Paul read aloud from Psalms.

'This day has been a miracle,' Christina whispered to her husband as they were alone together in bed. 'I can already see changes happening in Jerry.'

The next morning, breakfast was interrupted by Doc Cummings, who knocked hastily on the Coltens' front door. 'Little Connie Thompson just rode into town to get me,' the doctor explained to Paul. 'Says her pa is very sick and her ma is frantic with worry. I'm heading out to their ranch right now; thought you might want to come along, preacher.'

The problem at the Thompsons' turned out not to be serious. Doc Cummings accepted the invitation to stay for lunch, but Paul politely excused himself, saying, 'I need to get back to town.'

'I was only in town fer a few minutes this mornin',' Connie Thompson blurted out. 'But folks were jawin' 'bout you havin' Jerry Blaine stay in your home. I think it's a fine thing. After all, gunfighters are sinners too, right, Reverend Colt?'

Connie's mother began to correct her in regard to the pastor's name but he waved a hand to gently stop her. 'You're very perceptive, Connie.' Paul Colten laughed as he headed for the door of the ranch.

He wouldn't laugh again for a long time.

*

The moment Paul Colten had ridden back into town, he sensed something was wrong. People walking along the boardwalks seemed to deliberately look the other way as he rode down the main street. No one wanted their eyes to meet his.

Colten spurred his horse to a gallop. As he approached his house, he saw several people gathered outside. 'What's happened?' he shouted as he dismounted and tethered the animal. No one spoke.

Paul ran toward the front door. Sam Reynolds stepped from inside the house on to the small porch. His face was pale and contorted. 'Jerry Blaine, the son of my best friend, I can't believe. . . .'

'Believe what?' Paul shouted.

'He attacked her, attacked her hard. She fought back, but he was too strong for her. I'm so sorry, Paul.'

Colten ran into the house. Sam had placed a blanket over the body that lay on the floor. His hands trembling, Paul lifted the blanket, then gave out a tortured cry of despair that caused the group of people scattered about outside to first look down and then to hastily leave.

Sam Reynolds stayed but he didn't enter the house. Paul Colten needed some time alone. When the pastor finally stepped outside he was walking in a cautious, erect manner, as if in a slow-moving parade. Blood was smeared over him. Sam understood that the pastor had held his wife's body.

'When are we going after Blaine, Sheriff?'

'That's not the way to handle something like this, Paul. Jerry Blaine has at least two hours on us. He's got a fast horse and he knows how to cover his tracks.'

'Then just what do you intend to do, Sam?' An intense anger flamed through Colten's eyes and voice.

'Paul, you know what kind of man Jerry is—'

'Yes, Sam, I just found out what kind of man Jerry Blaine is! I used to have some very stupid notions about men like Jerry. Because of my stupidity, Christina is now dead.'

'Don't do this to yourself, Paul.'

'How are you going to find him, Sheriff?'

'Blaine is a troublemaker who likes to hang out in saloons. I'm telegraphing his name and description to every lawman hereabouts. He won't be hard to locate.'

The anger remained in Colten's eyes but his voice became a whisper. 'I'm going for the undertaker.' He quickly stepped off the porch.

Sam Reynolds shouted to the back of his friend. 'Paul, why don't you spend the night with Emma and me? We can pray together.'

Paul Colten stopped suddenly for a moment; he seemed unable to move. Finally, he looked back. 'No.' He turned his head and hastened away.

Christina had been buried the next morning. That afternoon, Zack Hogan rode into town. Paul Colten found the gunfighter standing at the bar in one of the town's better saloons.

'Mr Hogan?'

'Yes.' Zack Hogan stood a little on the short side. His beard was salt and pepper and his eyes were bloodshot. He had the look of a man who hadn't slept well in a long time.

'The name is Paul Colten. I want to hire you.'

The gunfighter's smile was sad and almost warm. 'Doesn't surprise me. I heard about what happened, preacher. I'm sorry.'

'Thanks. I want to hire you.'

'You want me to find Jerry Blaine and kill him.'

'I'm a selfish man, Mr Hogan. I want that pleasure for myself.'

'I don't understand. What—'

'I've hunted since I was a boy.' Colten's voice picked up speed and intensity. 'I know how to handle guns of all kinds, but I've never drawn against anyone. I want you to teach me. I'll pay well.'

Zack Hogan stared at the man in front of him. A gunfighter has to be able to read other men and what Hogan saw made him edgy, though he didn't show it. 'You don't want to do this, preacher. You're heading down a mean, lonely road. A road scattered with the dead. Right now, you may think you'll be able to go back and be what you once were. It never works that way.'

The words jolted the pastor. He realized that only two days ago he would have regarded Zack Hogan as being a man in need of redemption. He wondered if he would ever think like that again. Again, he said, 'I want to hire you.'

Zack Hogan had been a good teacher and in Paul Colten he had a very willing pupil. Hogan not only taught Colten the secrets of a fast, accurate draw but he also gave him some pointers on tracking – how to spot the tricks some men use to cover their trails.

After six weeks of instruction, Colten was holstering his gun after shooting four tin cans off a rock. 'Think I'm good enough to take on Jerry Blaine?'

'Don't know, never seen Blaine in action. But remember, he's a kid, still thinking about how fast he is. Keep your distance; his accuracy probably won't be that good.'

'Thanks, but Blaine is no kid. Not anymore. Sam was only half right. Blaine is easy to find but not to capture. He killed a deputy sheriff in Tucson last week and managed to elude a posse. I'm leaving town tomorrow afternoon. Going after him.'

The gunfighter looked confused. 'Why wait till afternoon?'

'Tomorrow is Sunday. I have to preach in the morning. It will be my final sermon. A friend from back East is on his way to take my place. I hope he does better than I did.'

Tracking Jerry Blaine had taken over twelve weeks. Blaine used his greatest weakness to some advantage. As Sam Reynolds predicted, Blaine spent a lot of time bragging about himself in bars. But he would also make declarations of where he was riding out to the next day. Colt came to realize the statements were a ruse to throw off whoever might be tracking him. At a small settlement in Texas, Colt found out Blaine had been there two days earlier boasting about taking over the town of Dallas.

Colt didn't head for Dallas. He picked up Blaine's trail outside the settlement. The kid was riding back to Arizona. 'Probably plans on making it to California,' Colt said to himself.

The sky was a fading red when Colt caught up with Blaine. The kid was hanging a coffee pot over a freshly built campfire. Blaine stood straight and watched with amused curiosity as the pastor rode toward him.

'Well, well, preacher man, are you still tryin' to save my soul?'

'No.' Colt dismounted and tethered his horse to a nearby tree.

'Then to what do I owe the pleasure of this visit?'

Colt took off his frock coat and tossed it over his saddle. Ignoring the advice of Zack Hogan, he walked toward his enemy until there were only a few yards between them. 'I'm here to kill you.'

Blaine laughed mockingly. 'Now, preacher, ain't there somethin' in the Good Book that says killing is wrong?'

A fierce rage surged through Colt as he stared at Blaine; rage that was directed at himself. Blaine was now wearing new, expensive clothes, but the sneer was still on his face and the voice was that of an animal that lived only to satisfy its most vicious desires. Colt wondered how he could have allowed a filthy monster like this to come into his home. How could he have been so wretchedly foolish as to leave Christina alone with such a loathsome piece of human garbage?

Colt had nothing more to say to this man. He continued to stare at him.

Something in that stare made Blaine nervous. 'Look, preacher man, I don't wanna kill ya. Sorry about your woman. I didn't wanna do it. Guess the Devil just gotta hold of me.'

Colt remained quiet.

'But I haven't forgot none about what you and your woman taught. I carry a Good Book with me everywhere. Got it in my saddle-bags right now.' He pointed toward the bags, which lay a few feet to his left, strewn over his saddle.

Colt turned his head slightly, pretending to look at the bags. That was enough to fool Blaine, who went for his gun. Blaine just had his silver-plated Smith & Wesson out of the holster when a bullet pierced his right shoulder. He screamed in pain and fired a shot into the ground as he staggered backwards.

Paul Colten had just shot a man for the first time. He experienced only an intense concentration on the moment.

'Oh please, preacher man, take me in if ya gotta but please don't. . . .'

Colt realized he had to act quickly. Jerry Blaine could drop the gun from his right hand at any time and he could never shoot an unarmed man. The former pastor suddenly felt he was at a pivotal point in his life. He could take Jerry Blaine in to the authorities, let the law handle it. That was the right thing to do, an act that would conform to everything he had preached from the pulpit.

Colt fired a second shot into Blaine's chest.

A numbness enveloped Paul Colten as he stood over Blaine's dead body. Paul had no idea how much time passed before he mechanically set about burying the corpse. Once Blaine was deep in the ground, Colt retrieved the gunfighter's horse, which he would later sell at a nearby settlement.

But he couldn't mount his own horse and ride off. Not yet. Blaine had lied about having a Good Book in his saddle-bags, but Colt had one in his. He couldn't leave until he performed a sacred duty.

Bible in hand, he slowly walked back to Blaine's grave. Colt's hands and forehead were now wet with perspiration. He dreaded this moment more than he had the gunfight. Once again standing over the grave of his enemy, Colt opened his Bible and began to read aloud the same psalm he had read on the night Christina had given Blaine a reading lesson.

Then came the hardest part. Paul Colten had not been able to pray since the day his wife was taken away from him. Christina, who should now be in Boston surrounded by a family that loved her, had been brutally murdered because her husband was a fool. A dangerous fool.

He needed to pray, to ask forgiveness, but no words came. The pastor couldn't speak about his wife, her murderer or himself. Paul Colten closed his eyes and hoped for a miracle, and then remembered what Christina had said about Blaine's first day with them: 'This day has been a miracle.'

Paul dropped to his knees and wept uncontrollably. It was the first time he had cried since that horrible day. His loud wails were quickly lost in the vastness of the encroaching night. The sky remained impassive as if the entire universe were indifferent to his pain. When the crying was finished, Colten felt no relief or comfort, only exhaustion. He gave up on praying, mounted his horse and rode off.

The boisterous sound of children laughing outside his hotel window returned Paul Colten to the present. He smiled, partly at the rambunctious shenanigans of the children below him and partly at the wisdom of Zack Hogan's words. The pastor had tried to go back to being what he had been, but it hadn't worked. Instead, he became a gunfighter himself.

He gently caressed the Bible lying on the table in front of him. His faith, though damaged, was still an important part of him. His Bible and his gun were both necessary for his own survival. That's why he liked the name 10-year-old Connie Thompson had given him a while back: 'Reverend Colt'.

'Pretty well sums me up,' he whispered to himself. He had come to Grayson, Texas to kill a man for money, a man that needed killing. But he was going to help some fine people who needed it. That, he would do for free.

He gathered up his notes and headed out of the hotel room. He needed to talk to Ox about a very important sermon.

CHAPTER NINE

The scene at the Mule Kick Saloon was joyous. Mandy Woods had started the Sunday morning service with two solos, which she sang while standing on the bar. Having completely won over the congregation, she asked them to join her for a performance of 'Swing Low, Sweet Chariot', challenging them to sing with even more pep than the crowd on Friday night. People gladly obliged, clapping and stomping their feet while they sang.

When she had finished, Ox sprang up from the first row, held Mandy's hand as she hopped down, then jumped on the bar himself. 'Thank you, Mandy! In all the times I've been at the Mule Kick, I've never seen so many happy, excited people. And all of you are sober!'

Ox paused for the laughter, then continued. 'Mandy will be up here singin' again, but first we're going to take us up a collection. Startin' this week, we are savin' up money to build a church.'

'I don't see the point, Ox,' a middle-aged man shouted from the third row back.

'Whaddya mean, Clarence?'

'Once the girl leaves, we will be back to the same dozen or so folks who usually come on Sunday morning. We don't need a fancy building for the few people who show up to listen to you.'

Ox pursed his lips, inhaled, and then spoke in an angry tone. 'Clarence, ya oughta know that building a church is part of makin' a town civilized. Now, I tend bar here at the Mule Kick and at Mr Hayworth's other saloon, the Lucky Aces. I know how ya gents spend your money and it won't hurt any of ya to give a dollar or two, or maybe even three, every week to build a church. And if ya fellas have any sense, you'll let this conversation end right here!'

Ox cleared his throat, primarily as an act to re-establish a more appropriate tone. 'I am now going to ask our ushers, Reverend Colt and Phineas Wilsey, to please come forward and pass the plates.'

As he passed the plate, Colt noted that the crowd was even larger than anticipated. Close to a hundred people were packed into the Mule Kick; there were families, ranch-hands, and several barflies who had slept outside the saloon so they wouldn't miss hearing Mandy sing.

The large crowd had necessitated that the service be conducted from atop the bar so that everyone could see and hear. The situation had not bothered Ox: 'The Apostles preached in the marketplace; I'll preach on top of a bar. Same thing, really.'

After the collection, Mandy sang *Amazing Grace*. Colt remembered the young woman saying she had sung in churches before. Her rendition of the hymn proved her statement. Mandy gave a beautiful and slow rendition of the song, getting the congregation in a more patient, reflective mood for the sermon.

Ox jumped onto the bar the moment Mandy departed, this time toting a Bible. He began his sermon by talking about David. 'Ya'll know about him, the shepherd boy who brought down Goliath with a slingshot. He did it by himself! Didn't need help from no one else, 'cept the Lord.

'But later, King Saul got it in his mind to kill David. This time, David didn't work alone. He got himself up an army – just like Saul's army. Now, we got us a similar problem right here in Grayson. There is a rancher in these parts who thinks he can kill at random—'

'This meeting is over right now!' Sheriff Lou Dixon shouted from where he stood behind the last row. 'You should have stuck with the pretty songs, Ox. I'm not allowing you to spout lies about—'

'It's the truth you're scared of, Dixon!' Ox slammed his Bible shut and pointed it at the sheriff as if it were a weapon. 'You ride out and tell Mr Caldwell he ain't runnin' this town. We're not scared of him no more.'

Lou Dixon sensed something dangerous in the room. People were nodding their heads in agreement with Ox and they didn't care if the sheriff saw them doing it. Dixon knew he had to back down for the moment.

Humiliation and anger combined in his voice. 'You should be scared, all of you! Ox has already been fired from one job. I suggest you people find another preacher. Someone who won't get you all killed.'

'I can't get fired this time.' Ox shrugged his shoulders in an elaborate manner. 'I ain't gettin' paid nothin'.'

The crowd laughed as Ox continued. 'Be sure and tell Mr Caldwell ta read the *Grayson Herald*. Read it ever' edition. There's gonna be plenty in there 'bout him. And I told our newspaper man to be sure and spell "Leonard Caldwell" right.'

Another round of laugher wavered across the Mule Kick. Phineas Wilsey wondered briefly if 'newspaper man' might become his nickname. Probably not. Too long.

Lou Dixon's anger was beginning to take on an element of fear. There was a threat in the air that he didn't know how to handle. He settled for a loud, contemptuous laugh and then hastily left the saloon, leaving the two batwing doors swinging wildly and squeaking loudly. The sound seemed to make some people edgy, as if it were an omen of more serious troubles ahead.

Ox sensed the nervousness. 'Now, I know you folks have a lot goin' on in your minds.' He pointed at his own head. 'Many of ya are probably wonderin' what's going on in my noggin, or if there is anything at all going on in there. Well, just listen. I'm gonna tell ya 'bout how we can be like David. We can form sort of an army of our own, help each other, protect each other, and make this a decent town to live in. Just give me fifteen minutes of your time. Well, maybe twenty-five. I'm gonna get started again by readin' my text. . . .'

Lou Dixon couldn't get the fear out of his system as he rode toward the Caldwell ranch. He had always known Caldwell was crazy. The guy kept jawing about building the biggest ranch in Texas. Hogwash. The Bar C wasn't anywhere near the biggest ranch in Texas. Never would be.

Dixon had been a hired gun in a few range wars. He knew Caldwell was lucky. There were no large spreads nearby to challenge him, just two-bit operations and some hardscrabble ranches.

Still, Leonard Caldwell had money, paid well, and so far the job hadn't been all that rough. As Dixon tied his horse to the hitch rail in front of Caldwell's ranch house, he wondered how long that situation would continue.

Donny quickly answered Dixon's knock but only opened the door a few inches. 'Good morning, Sheriff. How you do?'

'Mornin'. I need to talk with Caldwell, now.'

Lou started to enter but was blocked by a polite, smiling Donny. 'I tell Mr Caldwell. You wait here.' He closed the door, leaving Lou Dixon standing on the enclosed porch and cussing in a low whisper.

Donny moved cautiously toward the dining room. He hated Sundays, when his boss acted particularly strange. Mr Caldwell would spend a whole morning in the dining room talking to himself.

As Donny tapped on the dining room door, he heard his boss talking. 'I'm sure looking forward to the picnic this afternoon. . . .'

Donny stood outside the dining room and continued to listen. Apparently, his boss hadn't heard him, for Leonard Caldwell continued to talk: 'But we have to be careful about letting Rose eat too many berries. Remember what happened last time. . . .'

Donny tapped again, this time much louder. There was a sudden silence inside the dining room followed by an angry 'What is it?'

Cautiously, the young man opened the door. 'Excuse me, Mr Caldwell. Sheriff Dixon here. He says it very important.'

Leonard Caldwell stared into space as if trying to recollect who Sheriff Dixon was. As he slowly turned his head and looked at the portrait on the wall of his wife and daughter, his lips moved but no sound came out.

Caldwell suddenly bolted from his chair. He didn't speak to Donny until he was several steps out of the dining room. 'Where is he?'

'Outside, on porch.'

'Thank you.' The words were a dismissal. Donny gave a quick bow and hurried off to do work in the kitchen. He would work quietly while listening for angry words that could mean his boss was in trouble.

Leonard Caldwell made a few long strides to the front door and opened it with an angry swish. The rancher's eyes were no longer vague. He stared at his henchman with a stark coldness. 'What is it?'

'Mr Caldwell, I'm sorry, know you don't like to be bothered on Sunday, but—'

'What is it?'

Dixon looked about nervously. A few ranch-hands were walking by, engaged in casual conversation. 'We need to talk in private.'

Caldwell stepped back, allowing the crooked lawman to enter. 'There's no one around.' He closed the door. 'Now, what is so all-fired important?'

Lou Dixon gave a quick account of the meeting at the Mule Kick Saloon. Caldwell listened carefully, seeming to be most interested in Ox's remarks about the newspaper.

'What's got into that fool Easterner?' The rancher's voice sounded more incredulous than angry. 'He knows if I gave the word, no merchant in town would advertise in the *Herald*. They couldn't risk losing the Bar C business, except for—' An ugly smirk suddenly creased Caldwell's face. 'Hayworth. Stephen Hayworth! He'd give that Wilsey character the money to keep going.'

'I could smash up that newspaper office tonight, Mr Caldwell. Wilsey could disappear, never be seen—'

'No. We need to cut off the head of the snake.'

The rancher began to strut about his living room. The strangeness of both the man and the situation kept Lou Dixon edgy. The ranchers he had worked for in the past had officially given him a job as a ramrod, but Caldwell had made him a sheriff. His previous bosses looked upon other ranchers as their chief enemy. Caldwell had a bug in his ear about Stephen Hayworth, a guy who owned two saloons and a stable.

Of course, Hayworth was the only man around who could challenge Leonard Caldwell in the money department. Dixon suppressed a smile as he realized Hayworth owned the one business Caldwell couldn't control. There was no way the rancher could keep even his own ranch-hands from patronizing the two best saloons in town.

'We'll kill two birds with one stone.'

His boss's voice snapped Dixon from his musings. 'Ah, I don't follow you.'

As Leonard Caldwell explained his plan, Lou Dixon's nervousness subsided. Caldwell was crazy, but crazy like a fox. His plan was smart and would get rid of everyone who stood in his way. Tonight, Dixon knew he would earn his pay, but he had already been involved in plenty of killings and this one was particularly well planned. Lou Dixon left the ranch feeling good.

CHAPTER TEN

'So, I got nine men signed on to help.' Ox addressed a small group of people sitting around the living room of Stephen Hayworth's fine home, late Sunday night. 'These men will take turns at guarding ranches, businesses and other stuff owned by those folks who speak up against ol' Leonard. Got two men sawin' logs at the present time. They will spell Mr Hayworth and Reverend Colt in a few hours at the newspaper office. Got a third man outside this house right now. Miss Woods will stay here and nap for a while and then go back to the Noonan ranch.'

Ox looked carefully at the paper in front of him. 'What chicken scratched out this plan? I can't hardly read it. Oh yeah, it was me.' The former lawman looked at Colt. 'After you're done at the newspaper, you're ridin' back to the Noonan ranch with Miss Woods, then bringin' her back with you in the mornin', aren't ya?'

'Yes. I'll check with Tom and Joe about guarding the ranch at night. I'd be very surprised if they aren't already taking care of that.'

'Consider my father your tenth man,' Mandy Woods spoke up. 'He wanted to be here today for the services and all, but he and Tom Noonan are working hard at rounding up horses.'

Ox caught the apologetic tone in Mandy's voice. 'Don't worry at all about your pa not bein' here today. It says in the Good Book that a man can skip the Sabbath if his ox is in a pit. That applies to your pa and Tom Noonan.'

Phineas Wilsey decided on a bit of wordplay. 'I know of one Ox that Caldwell would like to put in a pit, but he'll never succeed.'

That line got smiles and a couple of laughs. Mandy was one of those who laughed, which was enough for Phineas.

'I got nothin' else to say, so I'll shut up. Gotta get to my job at the Mule Kick.' Ox glanced quickly at Stephen Hayworth and Colt. 'And you gents need to get to the newspaper office.'

As everyone stood up, Stephen Hayworth smiled at Mandy. 'Miss Woods, you will be perfectly safe here for the next few hours. Utah Benson will be guarding the house.' He pointed at the puffy sofa Mandy had just been sitting on. 'Make yourself comfortable or, if you prefer, I have a very large bed. You are welcome to sleep there.'

Hayworth's last statement had been offhand but seemed to embarrass him. He looked away from Mandy and then, appearing to need something to do, cleared his throat.

The young woman shared his uneasiness. She smiled and moved her hands in a flighty gesture. 'Ah, thank you, Mr Hayworth, the sofa will be fine. Just fine.'

'Good!' Hayworth replied in clipped, military fashion. 'Ah, gentlemen, we need to get to our posts.'

Colt's post was under a tree in a thin line of forest behind the stores of Grayson's Main Street. He wouldn't allow himself to lean against the tree. He was tired and afraid of falling asleep.

He gave a silent yawn as he looked at the back of the newspaper office and wondered if Phineas Wilsey was asleep inside. He hoped so. The hour was getting close to eleven. The newspaper man was going to need all the rest he could get.

Colt smiled as he recalled Phineas volunteering to watch the Hayworth house while Mandy Woods was sleeping inside. Ox had gently turned down the offer, then whispered to Colt, 'That would be like putting a rabbit in charge of the lettuce.'

Not really, Colt mused to himself. The gunfighter began to think about his early relationship with Christina, then tried to banish those thoughts.

The sound of intense whispers brought Colt back to the present. He stood completely still, his ears now picking up the words of the newcomers.

'You bring the matches?'

'Not here, stupid. This is the gun shop. The newspaper place is next door.'

'Oh.'

Colt recognized the voices: it was Mitch and Amos, the two lowlifes who had given Skeeter a hard time in the Mule Kick two nights before. He listened to their footsteps until they stopped only a few yards away from him. Mitch and Amos were now directly behind the office of the *Grayson Herald*.

'Now, you got the matches?' Amos held up a large stick he was carrying; the top was covered by rags.

'Just hold on.'

Colt stepped into the moonlight, gun in hand. 'Good idea, Mitch. Just hold on, both of you. Forget about setting a fire and put your hands up.'

Amos hurled the stick at Colt and both outlaws ran, apparently confident that Colt wouldn't shoot at them. They were right. Colt fired a shot into the air, then holstered his pistol and ran after the outlaws. He was catching up with them as they reached the gun shop. Stephen Hayworth, who had been watching the newspaper office from the front, moved stealthily around the far side of the shop and flattened himself against the back. Mitch and Amos didn't notice him until he stuck out one foot and tripped Mitch. The outlaw hit the ground and, in a motion that was almost graceful, Hayworth pulled out his Peacemaker and swung it against Mitch's head.

Amos kept running, but not for long. Colt tackled him and the two men went down. Amos tried to grab for his gun but was stopped by a hard slam from Colt's right fist.

Colt buoyed to his feet, took Amos's gun from its holster and pointed it at the outlaw. 'Get up, now!'

By the time Amos was upright, Stephen Hayworth had put Mitch through a similar routine. Both failed arsonists were now standing unsteadily on their feet.

'I'll take these fine citizens to the sheriff's office,' Colt said. 'You stay here and keep an eye on things.'

'Sheriff Dixon can be a very forgiving man at times.' There was a sharp edge to Hayworth's voice. 'Are you going to trust him to jail them?'

Colt gave a cynical smile. 'I'll make sure Dixon doesn't get carried away with his Christian charity.'

Deputy Harry Blackburn looked out the window of the sheriff's office and shouted nervously, 'He's coming, boss! That Reverend.'

'Get away from there!' Dixon spoke in a sharp whisper from where he sat at his desk. 'Look like you're doing something.'

Blackburn scurried over to the office's gun rack and pretended to be inspecting the rifles. The deputy's motions were awkward. Blackburn was good with a gun but excess weight on his medium frame often made him slow and clumsy. The deputy turned his head toward the front door as Colt entered with his two prisoners.

'I want these men jailed, Sheriff,' Colt demanded.

'Why?' Dixon asked. 'Because you say so?'

'Because they tried to burn down the newspaper office tonight.'

Sheriff Lou Dixon did not like Reverend Colt. The anger in his voice came naturally. 'And I suppose you just happened to be the only witness to this attempted crime.'

'Wrong. Stephen Hayworth was also there. He can testify against these men.'

Dixon leaned back in his chair. 'Well, well, now. That is quite a coincidence. Stephen Hayworth and Reverend Colt, two of the men who have been spreading lies about Leonard Caldwell, catch a couple of gents trying to set fire to the newspaper. Next, you'll say they were acting on Caldwell's orders.'

Colt wouldn't be goaded into riding off on a side trail. 'I want these men jailed. I'll be happy to—'

'OK, OK.' Dixon stood up and took the jail keys from the right-hand drawer in his desk. 'We can do the paperwork in the morning. Follow me.'

Keys jangling from one hand, the sheriff led the way into the jail area with Colt still keeping a gun pointed at the two prisoners. Harry Blackburn trailed behind. Colt frequently glanced back at him.

Dixon waved a hand around the room. 'All four cells are empty. Guess I can give both of our guests private accommodation.' The sheriff opened two cells and bowed in a mocking manner as Mitch and Amos each entered a cell. Dixon laughed as he locked the two prisoners inside. 'I think the newspaper will be safe for tonight. Is there anything else I can do for you, Reverend Colt?'

'These men had better stay here. I'll be back in the morning.'

'Looking forward to it, Reverend. Always happy to do everything I can for a visiting gunfighter.'

Colt and Lou Dixon exchanged hostile stares, then Colt

holstered his gun and slowly began to walk toward the door of the sheriff's office. Harry Blackburn followed behind him, trying to look officious.

'Let us out of here, Lou.' Mitch spoke in a low voice. 'My head hurts something awful.'

'Lay down and sleep it off, both of you. I want you jaspers out of the way for the rest of this night.'

Amos ran a hand lightly over his face, caressing the area where he had been punched. 'Do ya think Mr Caldwell will be mad at us for gettin' caught?'

'Don't see why.' Dixon's voice was jovial. 'He knew you boys would get nailed.'

Loud exclamations came from the jail cells. 'Quiet, both of you,' Dixon ordered. 'Just take it easy. Me, I got work to do.'

CHAPTER ELEVEN

Both Stephen Hayworth and Reverend Colt walked quietly toward the large sofa in Hayworth's living room. A needless courtesy since they were there to wake up Mandy Woods. Colt remained behind the sofa while Stephen stepped around to the front.

'Miss Woods,' the businessman said quietly.

The young woman stirred but did not wake up.

'Miss Woods,' he repeated.

Mandy opened her eyes and smiled. 'Time to go?' Her voice was soft and a touch uncertain.

Hayworth smiled and nodded his head.

The young woman stood up and without giving it any thought, did a long stretch. Watching her, Stephen Hayworth felt stunned by the feelings that coursed through him and quickly shifted his gaze to the floor. He wondered if Colt had noticed anything wrong in his demeanor but was too embarrassed to look at the former clergyman.

'Reverend Colt and I stopped by the livery and retrieved the horses.' Hayworth's eyes remained downward. His voice was heavy with a false casualness. 'They are outside.'

'Thanks. Both of you. Did everything go OK at the newspaper office?' Mandy had not noticed anything unusual about her host's behavior.

'Everything is fine,' Colt answered. 'I'll give you the details as we ride out to the Noonan place.'

'I wish I could say your carriage awaits, but I'm afraid we can't offer you anything that elaborate.' The businessman had wanted to say something funnier but that seemed to do. Mandy looked content enough as Stephen Hayworth followed her and Colt outside and waved them goodbye.

His guests weren't quite out of sight when Hayworth saw Utah Benson walking around to the front of his house. 'Just checking on the back, Mr Hayworth. Everything looks fine.'

Hayworth wondered how Utah could ever see anything. The man's thick hair was always disheveled and seemed to hang over his eyes.

'Thanks, Utah. Miss Woods has left now. You can go on home.'

'But—'

'I can take care of myself.'

'Well, Ox couldn't get no one to spell me tonight and I gotta open the store early as always, so, if you're sure?'

'I'm sure, now get on home and get to bed.'

After closing the front door of his home, Hayward walked over to a cabinet in his living room. The time had arrived for his evening brandy and cigar.

As he poured the drink, Hayworth reflected on the fact that the day had been an important one in the life of the town. He was proud to be part of a group that was trying to make Grayson a decent place. Yes, the day had gone well. People had responded enthusiastically to Ox's sermon and. . . .

Taking a cigar from an ornate box, Hayworth laughed out loud and looked down at the floor. There was no one there to see it but his face was red. He carried the smoke and drink to his easy chair and sat down.

As he inhaled on the cigar, Hayworth admitted to himself that the best part of his day had been the few minutes he had spent alone with Mandy Woods. They had discussed music, as both were self-taught on the guitar.

'You are a much better musician than I am, Miss Woods. If I had been playing and singing this morning, the Mule Kick would have emptied out quickly.'

'Maybe we can do a duet some Sunday, Mr Hayworth,' Mandy had replied. For a few moments, the young woman's wonderful smile had been aimed entirely at him.

Stephen Hayworth tapped his cigar on a large ashtray that sat on a side table beside his chair. He would never sing, of course, but he would enjoy playing the guitar with Mandy.

A haze of smoke surrounded the businessman as he continued to struggle with his thoughts and emotions. He had to be careful not to make an old fool of himself. After all, he was old enough to be Mandy's father. And he had no illusions. Mandy had no romantic interest in him and never would. All he really hoped for was a little time with the girl, time when he could enjoy her company. Nothing more.

Hayworth sipped his brandy and reflected on why he had never married. The answer wasn't hard to come by. There had never been many women in his life, for one thing. He had been in his early twenties when the war between the states ended. He had remained in the Union army and been assigned to a fort in the West. There were not many women around, and plenty of competition for the few that were available.

'I quit the army to get rich,' Hayworth said to himself in a low voice. 'Guess I succeeded.' The businessman took another sip of brandy, and then met his own eyes reflected in a glass-fronted cabinet. 'Oh, stop feeling sorry for yourself.'

He picked up a copy of *Great Expectations* which lay beside the ashtray on the side table and began to read. An hour later, he put the book aside and again spoke out loud. 'Maybe I should practice on the guitar before going to bed. I'll never be as good as Mandy Woods, but if I accompany her I'll need to get better. . . .'

There was a knock on the front door. Embarrassment again washed over Stephen Hayworth. Had the person outside heard him talking to himself about Mandy Woods?

No. His chair was far from the front door and he had been talking in a low voice. Hayworth cleared his throat, got up and walked slowly to the door. As he did so, he naturally regained his military bearing.

When he opened the front door, Hayworth recognized the man standing on his porch as a henchman of Leonard Caldwell's. 'Yes?'

'Mr Hayworth, I work for Leonard—'

'I know that! What do you want?'

Phil Varden held up a hand in something of a peace gesture. 'Mr Caldwell knows all about the meetin' at the Mule Kick this morning. He don't want any more trouble. Thinks maybe you and he can work out some sort of peaceable arrangement.'

'Then, why isn't Caldwell here?'

'Well, he sent this letter first.' Varden held up an envelope. 'Wants you to read it and tell me whatcha think. I'll take the message back to him.'

Hayworth took the envelope and ripped it open, not noticing that Phil Varden's eyes darted about, ensuring that no one else was nearby. The letter inside had been folded several times and it took him a moment to work through those folds. 'There's nothing written on this paper at all. . . .'

Stephen Hayworth silently cursed his own carelessness. How could he have fallen for this? He hastily turned toward the gunman standing on his porch but it was too late. Hayworth never even saw the gun, only heard the explosion and felt the terrible burning sensation as he staggered back into his house and collapsed, writhing in pain on the floor.

He was dying. He'd never get a chance to play the guitar with Mandy Woods. It was one of the few things he had looked forward to in a long time and now it would never happen. He had only himself to blame; he never should have fallen for such an obvious trick.

Another shot fired and Stephen Hayworth's body went still.

Ox was tired, but restless. He stacked the last of the chairs on a table and prepared to clean the floor of the Mule Kick. Sunday was always the deadest night for both saloons, which pleased Ox. His Sundays started even earlier than the other six days.

There was a poker game still going on at the Lucky Aces but, from what the barkeep there told him, it wasn't an all-night affair. After cleaning up at the Mule Kick, he would go over to the Lucky Aces and do the same, then lock up the money and receipts.

Ox had gotten started with the broom when Dutcher Poston entered the saloon. 'Need to talk to you, Ox.'

Ox stopped sweeping. 'You've never been much inclined to strike up a conversation with me before, Dutcher; why the sudden change?'

'There's somethin' you need to know about.'

'Yeah. What's that?'

'I saw a suspicious-looking character hanging around Stephen Hayworth's house.'

'When?'

'Just now. I figured with Mr Hayworth being your boss and all, you'd want to know.'

'Bein' a good citizen is kind of a new thing for ya, ain't it, Dutcher?'

'Look, I jus' came in here to tell you what I saw! Your boss may be in danger. If that don't interest you none, fine.' Dutcher stomped out of the Mule Kick.

Suspicion coursed through the ex-lawman. Something about this wasn't right. Still, Mr Hayworth could be in danger. Ox dropped the broom and hurried behind the bar where he retrieved his holster. He was still strapping it on as he hustled outside the saloon and began a fast walk to Stephen Hayworth's home where he had been only a few hours before.

Ox slowed his pace slightly in order to make less noise. If someone was prowling outside the Hayworth house, he didn't want to scare him off; better to capture him and find out what all of this was about.

A gunshot from Hayworth's house shattered all such thoughts and spurred Ox into a fast run.

As he got into sight of the house, he saw that the front door was open. Ox heard another shot. He looked about for Utah Benson but couldn't spot him. As he ran into the Hayworth home he heard the sound of frantic hoofbeats coming from behind the house, and saw Stephen's body on the floor. He crouched and quickly placed a finger on Stephen Hayworth's neck, confirming his worst fears.

Ox sprang up and ran toward the fluttering curtains on the back wall of the house. A large window was wide open. The killer had tied his horse up behind the house and then—

'Turn around slow, Ox. Real slow, with your hands up.'

Ox did what he was told and found himself facing Lou Dixon. 'I smelled a rat. Guess I should say rats. Caldwell had Stephen Hayworth murdered and now you're gonna hang me for doin' it.'

Dixon laughed; he was enjoying himself. 'You're right, Ox. Dead right.'

CHAPTER TWELVE

Donny awoke suddenly, his mind groggy. He listened carefully for a repetition of the noise that had startled him from a deep sleep.

'Help! I'm being beaten to death!'

The voice belonged to his boss, but the tone was all wrong. He sounded almost playful. But then, panic can affect the way a man sounds.

'Help! Help!'

Donny bolted from the bed, put on a robe, and moved stealthily from his room beside the kitchen. Moving into the kitchen, he grabbed a meat cleaver from a rack on the wall and nudged open the door that connected to the house's large dining room. The room was empty.

'Somebody help me! I'm doomed!'

With a few quick steps, Donny crossed the large dining room and partially opened the door that led to the living room. One lamp was on. His boss was lying on the floor.

'Help me, Jeannie. This little ball of fire is about to trample me to death!'

Donny hastily pulled back the door until there was only a crack through which he could watch Leonard Caldwell. The man was now laughing and obviously in no danger, or at least not the kind of danger where a meat cleaver would be of any help.

The cook reentered the kitchen and, for a moment leaned against a wall and listened to his boss's insane babble. 'Oh, now she is pulling my nose off. Help me, Jeannie! Don't just sit there laughing!'

Donny placed the meat cleaver back in its rack. This was not the first time something like this had happened. From listening in on previous occasions when Leonard Caldwell retreated into a different world, the cook knew that 'Jeannie' was the name of his employer's deceased wife and 'Rose' was the name of their child who had died a few months before her mother's passing.

'Oh, she has decided to show me a touch of mercy. . . .'

A blade of moonlight cut through the kitchen window. The night was warm, but Donny's entire body shivered as if he were in a blizzard. He wanted to run far away from this house, find a job as a cook in one of the larger towns. He would save his money and, some day, have a restaurant of his own.

But he was beholden to Leonard Caldwell. The man had saved his life and then given him a job.

'I think our little ball of fire is getting tired. Maybe she needs a nap before we go on our picnic.'

Donny's eyes rested upon the dark shapes of the kitchen. His boss was sinking deeper and deeper into insanity. In the past, Leonard Caldwell had talked to his dead loved ones, but always while sitting alone in the dining room at breakfast time. Now, he was in the living room acting out his illusions.

'Jeannie, this ranch is on its way to being the biggest ranch in Texas. I want you to know that I'm doing it all for you and our daughter.'

Donny quietly returned to his bedroom, but he didn't sleep for the rest of the night.

CHAPTER THIRTEEN

'I think love is the most powerful force in the world, don't you, Reverend Colt?' Mandy Woods spoke as she and Colt were riding back into town from the Noonan ranch.

When her companion didn't reply, Mandy felt uneasy and added, somewhat defensively, 'The Good Book has a lot to say about love.'

'That's right, Miss Woods. But remember, evil is a very powerful force, too.

'You don't think evil is as powerful as love, do you?'

Colt wasn't enjoying this conversation, but felt obligated to be honest with the young woman. He didn't want to attack her idealism, but Mandy Woods couldn't afford to be naïve. A naïve person couldn't survive for long in the West.

'The Good Book also has a lot in it about evil,' the former clergyman said. 'Unfortunately, folks don't pay enough attention to that part. Evil isn't as strong as love, but it fights hard and cruel. And it never really surrenders. Every morning, you have to get up and fight it again.'

Mandy Woods busied herself with her horse's reins. Colt could see that she was thinking over his words. He hoped he had done her some good.

Colt became tense as they rode into Grayson. Something was

wrong. People were too quiet, ignoring him and Mandy and each other. This reminded him of that terrible day when he returned to his home to find. . . .

Colt and Mandy tied up their horses in front of the *Herald* office. The young woman didn't seem to notice anything wrong and Colt tried not to show his anxiety as they stepped inside.

The scene inside the *Herald* only heightened Colt's tension. Lou Dixon seemed to be lecturing Phineas. The sheriff turned his head toward the newcomers. 'Reverend Colt, it's right nice of you to bring some help for Phineas. He's gonna be pretty busy, reporting on all the sad events that took place last night.'

Colt stared at the lawman, but said nothing.

'Guess you haven't heard.' Dixon made no attempt to keep the delight out of his voice. 'Stephen Hayworth was murdered last night, right in his own home.'

Colt remained still but Mandy inhaled and placed a hand on her chest.

'Yeah, young lady, it's a terrible thing. But don't worry, we got the killer jailed.'

'Who might that be?' Colt spoke in an accusing voice.

'Ox.'

'That's impossible!' Mandy screamed. 'Ox and Mr Hayworth were friends. Mr Hayworth trusted Ox—'

'Yeah, it's pretty awful when a man turns on someone who trusted him; only a real snake would do something like that.' Dixon walked toward the front door of the *Herald*. 'But the circuit judge will be in town next week and Ox will hang for what he did. We have two eyewitnesses who will testify against him.'

Mandy started to say something but Colt squeezed her arm and she stifled her words.

Lou Dixon opened the door and turned toward Colt. 'With Stephen Hayworth gone, I'm afraid you got no case against

Mitch and Amos. I turned them loose a few hours ago.' He turned his gaze toward Phineas. 'Don't forget our little talk.' Grayson's sheriff stepped on to the boardwalk and slammed the door behind him.

Mandy ran toward Phineas, stopping a few inches from him. 'What happened, what—'

'It's true, Mr Hayworth was murdered and they have arrested Ox.'

'But you know Ox didn't do it!' Mandy's voice remained vehement.

'I know.'

The resignation in Phineas's voice worried Colt. He stood beside Mandy and spoke to the editor in a calm voice. 'What did Dixon mean by "our little talk"?'

'The sheriff wants me to help spread the word.' The quiet passivity remained in Phineas's voice. Colt realized that the young man was grieving the loss of a friend. 'There's going to be a meeting at noon today for all of the men in Grayson, at the Mule Kick. Leonard Caldwell is going to speak.'

'Is that all?' Colt prodded the journalist.

'Well, the sheriff did say he expects the paper to be fair in its coverage of the murder.'

'What does he mean by "fair"?' Mandy asked.

'We know the answer to that question.' Colt began to pace about the office, grief and rage coursing through him. 'Leonard Caldwell will decide what is fair.'

Mandy Woods cupped a hand over her face. 'Yesterday everything seemed so wonderful. Now, Mr Hayworth, that fine, fine man, has been murdered, Ox is in jail and—'

'What were we just talking about, Miss Woods?'

The young woman brushed off a few tears, then moved her hand away from her face. 'I don't understand, Reverend Colt.'

'Evil is powerful.' Colt's voice was almost a shout. 'Powerful, ruthless and unpredictable. And it never plays by the rules.'

Phineas Wilsey gave a sardonic laugh. 'Evil doesn't observe proper etiquette.'

'Good line.' Colt gave the journalist a hard look. 'Use it in an editorial.'

'I plan to, and there is plenty to editorialize about.'

'What do you mean?' Mandy asked.

'I've been on this story since early this morning,' Wilsey proclaimed in a dramatic fashion. He was obviously showing off for the young lady, but Colt regarded that as a positive sign.

Phineas continued: 'There are two so-called eye witnesses who claim that they saw Ox shoot Stephen Hayworth from his front porch: Phil Varden and Dutcher Poston. Both are gunslicks working for Leonard Caldwell. No one is going to believe their stories.'

'No one believed that Sheriff Russ Jones accidentally killed himself while cleaning his gun, either,' Colt said. 'But not enough people would speak up.'

Colt took a few steps toward the front door of the office, then turned around to face Mandy and Phineas. 'You two stay here and work on those editorials. I'm going to visit Ox and make sure he is safe, at least for the moment. Then I'm going to check on those nine men Ox had lined up and see how many are still with us. Some of them will be assigned to this office.'

'I can protect the newspaper office!' Phineas spoke in a strident manner.

The last thing Colt wanted to do was to embarrass Phineas in front of Mandy. 'I know you can. But you'll have to leave this place to investigate the murder. The newspaper is an obvious target. We can't be too careful. See you at noon in the Mule Kick. And one more thing.'

Colt paused for a moment; several moments, in fact. Phineas finally prodded him with a 'Yes?'

'That attack on the newspaper office last night was phony.' Anger streaked Colt's face. 'Caldwell knew we'd relax a bit after stopping those two thugs.'

Phineas understood Colt's reasoning. 'That made it easier for him to carry out the real plan – to murder Mr Hayworth.'

'The bad ones never take time off,' Colt said. 'From now on, we won't either.'

The atmosphere inside the saloon was edgy. Men were trying to joke and act casual, but the good cheer was obviously forced.

'This could be my last day here.' George spoke to Colt and Phineas as he brought them their beers. 'With Mr Hayworth gone, I don't know who is paying me, or if anyone is.' He turned to take care of other customers.

'So, how many men do we still have with us?' Phineas asked as he sipped his drink.

'All nine. Utah Benson over at the mercantile is especially upset. Feels guilty about leaving Hayworth alone. He says Hayworth insisted that he go, and I believe him. From now on Utah will advertise in the *Grayson Herald* and sell it at his store. It's not just the guilt. Ox's preaching really got to him yesterday.'

'I need to visit Ox this afternoon—'

Phineas's words were cut short by a loud stir, which skimmed across the Mule Kick as Leonard Caldwell stepped into the saloon. Caldwell was accompanied by Lou Dixon and a short, stocky man Colt recognized.

'Isn't that the mayor?'

Phineas nodded his head. 'His Honor, Mayor Horatio Camrose. He is also the town's only lawyer.'

Caldwell shook a few hands, slapped a few backs, then stood up on a table. 'Men, I have something important to say. I'll be short and to the point.'

Caldwell paused as Horatio Camrose stood on one side of the table, smiling in an ingratiating manner. On the other side stood Lou Dixon, looking at the crowd with eyes that were cold and threatening.

'Last night a citizen of Grayson was brutally murdered. Fortunately, the killer was quickly apprehended, thanks to Sheriff Lou Dixon!'

A moment passed before the crowd in the saloon realized they had just been handed an applause line. After a listless round of clapping, Caldwell continued. 'Some of you men know that Stephen Hayworth and I didn't see eye to eye on a lot of matters. But we respected each other and were friends.'

Reverend Colt and Phineas Wilsey exchanged curious expressions. Neither man knew where Caldwell's talk was leading.

The rancher pointed to the mayor standing on his right. 'This morning, Mr Horatio Camrose informed me that Stephen Hayworth left both of his saloons and the livery to me.'

A silence fell over the Mule Kick, a silence borne of fear. No one believed that Hayworth had left anything to Leonard Caldwell. The two saloons were the town's most prosperous enterprises. With Hayworth gone, Caldwell was now making his hold on Grayson, Texas complete.

Leonard Caldwell sensed the wariness that surrounded him. He saw the mayor fidgeting nervously and watched Lou Dixon tense up as his right hand moved closer to his gun. This wasn't the way the rancher wanted it. There was almost a pleading quality to his voice when he spoke again. 'My family and I want you to know that the Mule Kick and the Lucky Aces saloons will continue to serve the citizens of Grayson well.' He cleared his throat, then followed a sudden whim. 'To prove what I just said, for the next hour all the drinks at the Mule Kick and the Lucky Aces will be on the house. Enjoy yourselves, men!'

There was harsh, frantic cheering, as men rushed toward the bar. Colt and Phineas slowly advanced through the mob and out of the door. They quickly stepped off the boardwalk to avoid the throng that was running toward the Lucky Aces in order to be the first in line there.

There was another, much smaller scattering of men leaving the Mule Kick. These men carried looks of resignation. Caldwell was now in complete control of Grayson, and they could do nothing about it. Colt was relieved to see that none of the nine men in their unofficial army were a part of this group.

The gunfighter and the newspaper man stood in the road, a little past the hitch rail, to watch the commotion both inside and outside the saloon. Wilsey spoke in a mockingly cheerful voice. 'Well, I know of one story that will run in the Saturday edition of the *Grayson Herald*.'

'What's that?'

'Why, the Sunday service. There's going to have to be a new preacher and a new location.'

Colt, Phineas and Mandy stepped into the sheriff's office and saw a very sullen-looking deputy sitting at the desk.

Colt instantly understood the source of Harry Blackburn's discontent. 'Good afternoon, we are here to visit the prisoner.'

'The sheriff says no visitors.' The deputy growled his response.

Colt smiled in a conspiratorial manner. 'I say that if Lou Dixon wants to enforce a crazy rule, he should come back from the Mule Kick, enforce it himself, and let you enjoy a free drink or two before the hour is over.'

The deputy gave a joyless laugh, then motioned with his thumb toward the jail cells.

Of the four cells, three were empty. Ox was sitting in one cell, on a battered cot. He got up and greeted his visitors. 'Always appreciate company. I'm a little short on ways to pass the time right now.' He gave a goofy smile. His humor was aimed at comforting Mandy Woods, whose face was pale and close to tears.

Colt wanted to talk with Ox while the revelry was still going on. He explained to the former lawman what had just happened in the Mule Kick.

'Caldwell says Stephen Hayworth left the saloons to him?!' Ox gave a long sigh and shook his head. 'I told Mr Hayworth not to trust Camrose, but he's the only lawyer in town and Mr Hayworth saw no trouble in havin' him draw up his will.'

'Did Stephen Hayworth discuss his will with you?' Colt asked.

'Sure did.'

'When?'

' 'Bout six months ago when he wrote it.'

'Why did he talk about it with you?'

' 'Cause he left me the two saloons – along with the livery.'

Ox's three visitors all gave various exclamations of shock. The former deputy smiled and continued. 'Surprised me, too. But Mr Hayworth had no family and said I was one of the few men in town that he trusted. Stephen Hayworth cared a whole lot about this town and its future.'

'Keep this quiet for a while, Ox.' Phineas spoke in an anxious whisper. 'Hayworth left you three very valuable properties. That gives you a motive for his murder.'

The big man nodded his head. 'That thought has occurred to me.'

'Horatio Camrose would have told Caldwell what was in that will.' Colt was almost talking to himself as much as he was to Ox. 'But Caldwell's not using that information to frame you.'

Ox shrugged his shoulders. 'Guess Caldwell figures he doesn't need it. He's got the part 'bout hangin' me pretty well sewed up. This way, Leonard Caldwell gets rid of a pest and gets two saloons and a livery into the bargain. Give the devil his due, it's a pretty good plan.'

'Yes, but the plan is flawed,' Colt replied. 'There would have been two copies of the will. Camrose, the lawyer, had one; Stephen Hayworth would have had the other. Any idea where he would have kept it?'

Ox didn't have to think very long on that one. 'It would be in his safe at the Mule Kick.'

'Hayworth had an office there?'

'Yeah. There's a door to the left of the bar. The bartender's left. It opens up to a very small hallway. At the end of the hall is Hayworth's office.'

'Caldwell will have to get to the safe very soon, probably tonight.' Colt looked down, appearing to retreat into himself, then once again faced Ox. 'Do you know the combination to the safe?'

Ox shook his head. 'My boss was a very private man. I suspect he kept that combination in his head and nowhere else. At closin', after I cleaned up the places, I would lock up the receipts and the cashboxes from both saloons in Hayworth's desk. I don't know what he kept in the safe, but it seems a likely place for the will.'

From the office area, they could hear Lou Dixon arriving. 'Too bad you had to miss out on the fun, Deputy. But don't worry, I drank your free drinks for you.'

Colt looked toward the office and then back at the prisoner. 'We should be going. Don't worry, we'll get you out of here, Ox.'

'Is there anything we can do for you in the meantime?' Mandy's face contorted as she spoke. Those were the first words she had been able to speak since entering the jail area.

Ox looked uneasy. 'Well, yeah, I'd appreciate it if you'd bring me some food—'

'Don't they feed you here?' Phineas asked.

'Sure do. And Lou Dixon or one of his deputies always spits on it just before they give it to me. Gives them a few laughs. Doesn't do much for my appetite.'

'That's outrageous!' The fire in Phineas's eyes was genuine. 'Mandy and I will go over to Gosden's Restaurant right now and bring you back a plate of food.'

There were a few more hasty goodbyes, and then the three-some left the cell area and entered the office where Lou Dixon now occupied the desk. The sheriff's eyes were glassy and his voice louder than usual. 'So, Ox still has three friends left in this town!'

'His friends intend to bring him three square meals a day!' Phineas's voice was also loud. 'And we are going to carry the food right to him. If you or any of your deputies try to stop us, it will be on the front page of the *Grayson Herald*. And, don't worry, I'll spell your name right.'

An hour of free drinks had left Lou Dixon careless with his words. 'You be careful, newspaper man. There's lots of things that can catch fire in a newspaper office. Why, a fire could break out while you were inside, with no chance to escape.'

'You be careful, Sheriff.' Phineas's voice piled sarcasm on to the official title. 'There are plenty of people in this town who are getting fed up with crooked lawmen.'

Phineas took Mandy's arm and walked out of the office. Colt trailed behind, stopping at the door and turning back to Lou Dixon. 'Better listen to what the man says. Remember, the pen is mightier than the sword.' He exited to a flurry of loud curses.

Outside on the boardwalk, Phineas had one arm around Mandy, who was crying into a handkerchief. She dabbed at her eyes for a moment. Her voice was wavy when she spoke. 'I understand better what you were saying about evil, Reverend Colt.'

Phineas gave Colt a questioning glance.

'I don't have a pulpit anymore, but I still preach occasionally,' Colt said. That gave both Mandy and Phineas a slight but much-needed laugh. Mandy used the occasion to discreetly move out from under her comforter's arm.

'I'll accompany you to Gosden's,' Colt said and the threesome began the short walk to the restaurant. 'Ox is a fine man. I want to have a hand in seeing that he's properly fed.' There was more to it than that. Phineas Wilsey had acquired a new determination to do what was right, a very welcome development. But the journalist was unarmed and not used to dealing with hardcases. Lou Dixon, a dangerous man under any circumstances, had been drinking. Colt wanted to be around if there was trouble delivering Ox's lunch.

As they walked together, Colt noticed that Mandy's tears had vanished and she also seemed to be experiencing a new determination to do what was right, or perhaps it would be more accurate to say that the old determination had returned.

The former clergyman's mind turned to other matters. 'Phineas, does Leonard Caldwell have any family that lives nearby?'

'No. Shortly after I arrived in Grayson, Mr Caldwell invited me to dinner at his home in order to talk about the newspaper.' The journalist cleared his throat, embarrassed by his former connection to a man he was now opposing. 'There is a portrait in Caldwell's dining room of him with his wife and daughter. But the portrait is at least ten years old and Caldwell told me he had lost both the wife and daughter long ago.'

'Why do you ask?' Mandy's voice was now firm.

'During his talk at the Mule Kick, Caldwell referred to "my family and I".' Colt looked directly at Phineas. 'You heard it, didn't you?'

'Yeah, it impressed me as a little strange.'

'I thought it was strange, too,' Colt said.

CHAPTER FOURTEEN

Colt sipped his drink slowly and spoke to the bartender at the Mule Kick. 'Long day, George?'

'Yeah, they're all gonna be long for a while. Ox is in jail and so far the new owner hasn't hired anyone to replace him. I'm having to tend bar, order the hooch, keep the books, you name it.'

Colt leaned against the bar and nodded at a table behind him. 'Maybe that game will break up soon and you can close and get some shut-eye.'

George shook his head. 'I know those gents. They'll be here to see the sun come up.' He pulled out his pocket watch. 'It's a little past one now, so I got another five hours until my replacement arrives at six.'

Deputy Harry Blackburn hastily entered the saloon, walked past the bar and stepped through the door that led to what was once Stephen Hayworth's office. The crooked lawman didn't notice Colt. George looked uneasy. Colt figured the bartender knew something crooked was going on, but had no idea what.

A few minutes later Lou Dixon stepped out of the office area and then quickly stepped back. Colt pretended not to see him. He took a final gulp of his drink, then spoke to George. 'Guess I'd better get some sleep. Going out to the Noonan place

103

tomorrow to help them round up some horses.'

Colt left the saloon and walked directly to the Grayson Hotel. Only once did he do a quick, partial turn of his head. That move was enough to confirm his suspicions.

He entered the lobby, exchanged a few words with the desk clerk and headed for his room. Once there, he struck a match and made his way to the brass lamp, which rested on a table beside the bed. He raised the chimney, touched a flame to the wick and replaced the chimney. The lamp tossed a glow on the curtains of the window that looked out on the street. After ten minutes, he extinguished the flame. He sat in the dark for another ten minutes, then left the hotel through a back door.

That should satisfy the sheriff, he thought.

A half hour later, Colt was once again in the thin strip of woods that ran behind the Main Street buildings. Only now, he was directly behind the Mule Kick. He noted that the wide path between the saloon and the woods had been cleared of the usual barflies, who would be sleeping it off at this time in the morning. The former clergyman figured the local law had taken care of that situation for reasons that had nothing to do with public order.

His suspicions were quickly confirmed. A thudding sound of hoofbeats and the clatter of a wagon began to sound from not too far away. The wagon, pulled by four horses, stopped behind the saloon. Three men jumped off and entered the back door of the Mule Kick.

Within a few minutes the men were coming out the back door of the saloon, toting a heavy object. Colt could hear whispered curses in a familiar voice. Following a string of obscenities, Lou Dixon continued his complaints.

'Careful! What are you doing, Mitch? I swear you're as useless as Harry.' Once the safe was in the wagon bed and covered by a blanket, Lou and Mitch ran around to the front of the Mule Kick while Harry Blackburn hastily got back on the seat of the wagon. The wagon lurched forward. Colt figured Lou and Mitch were mounting their horses, which would be tied to the hitch rail in front of the saloon.

Colt didn't have to hurry toward his own horse, which was tied nearby. He wasn't worried about following the wagon or being spotted. Leonard Caldwell, his cronies and his henchmen had become too confident; one of their few weak spots.

Besides, Colt knew exactly where the wagon was headed. He took the trail that led to Caldwell's ranch and remained a good distance behind the dilapidated contraption carrying a safe containing papers that could send Leonard Caldwell to jail.

As he rode, the gunfighter reflected on the changes he had seen in Phineas Wilsey over the last few hours. There was a new determination in the man that went beyond trying to impress Mandy Woods.

Learning Ox's jailers had been spitting in his food had put a real fire in the newspaper man. Phineas had to have heard about the men, women and children that Leonard Caldwell had killed and, of course, there was the murder of Stephen Hayworth.

Somehow, Phineas had been able to diminish those events in his mind and deny what was happening all around him, but when a good friend, Ox, told him about the way his food was ruined, the scales at last dropped from the young man's eyes. Phineas realized the evil he was confronting. He would risk everything to bring Caldwell's empire down. Colt looked at the surrounding stars and hoped that Phineas and Mandy would be careful about every step. 'Don't let any harm come to them,' he whispered aloud to the sky. It was the closest he had come in some time to praying.

As the wagon pulled up beside Caldwell's large home, Colt

left the trail, tied his horse and advanced toward the ranch on foot. His first stop was a large bunkhouse, where he could hear the assorted snores and mumblings of sleeping men. He dashed from the bunkhouse to a storage shed. The shed was located near the bunkhouse and several yards to the side of the ranch house, giving Colt a good view of Caldwell's living quarters.

The gunman spotted slivers of yellow light, which he judged to be spraying out from a back window, near the far end of the house. He figured that room might be an office where Caldwell took care of his paperwork.

Colt wanted to get closer, but it would be risky. There was no cover between the shed and the house. Bending over in a jack-knife position, he moved quickly to the ranch house and pressed his body against a side wall. He could hear voices coming from the open window but couldn't make out what they were saying. He moved cautiously around to the back of the house and stopped near two fluttering curtains, where he could hear angry voices engaged in an argument of some kind.

Caldwell's voice was immediately recognizable. 'You did follow my instructions, didn't you, Lou? Beau Toomey is arriving on the train tomorrow at five.'

'Yeah, I did, Leonard.' Lou Dixon's voice resounded with the anger of a man who didn't like to think of himself as a lowly servant who did the king's bidding.

'Well then, there is nothing to worry about, everything is going as I—'

As Caldwell spoke, Colt thought he heard footsteps coming from . . . somewhere. The gunman drew his revolver and eyed the surrounding darkness. He couldn't spot a thing but remained alert for any movement or sound.

'But we don't need no safecracker!' Dixon's voice became louder. 'Let's blow the safe open right now. If the will gets burned up, so what? You want it destroyed anyhow!'

'Stephen Hayworth was my enemy,' Leonard Caldwell whipped back. 'I need to read all the papers in that safe, know everything Hayworth was up to. He might have been in cahoots with someone who passes himself off as a friend!'

'OK, OK.' Lou Dixon sighed and uttered a few curses.

'There will be no language like that used in this house!' Caldwell's anger was becoming ferocious. 'There is a lady and child present.'

'What?'

'Get out! Now! Get out!'

Dixon and his companions weren't the only ones who needed to leave. Colt eyed the area around him carefully and once again moved through the darkness, this time away from the house. He became very cautious as he passed the shed, but nothing happened.

The gunman wondered if he had really heard anything or if his imagination had gotten the best of him.

Donny watched the stranger vanish into the night, then leaned against the shed and sighed with relief. He would not have to use the knife, which remained in his right hand.

The young man knew that only a year ago he would have attacked the intruder immediately. No more. He now realized that Leonard Caldwell was a dangerous lunatic who surrounded himself with evil men.

But Mr Caldwell had saved his life, given him a job and treated him well. Surely, he owed the man a debt.

Donny thought about his father and wondered what advice he would give, but his father was far away. Donny felt very alone.

CHAPTER FIFTEEN

Phineas Wilsey looked at Mandy Woods, who rode only a few feet away to his left side. She was perfect, absolutely perfect. He wanted so badly to say something to her but couldn't think of a thing. He had dreamed of having time alone with her. Now that time had arrived and he wanted nothing more than to be in town and at the newspaper office where he could hide behind his work.

Nothing seemed to make sense anymore! He had been excited when Colt had asked him to ride back to the Noonan Ranch with Mandy and spend the night there, then ride back with her in the morning. But during the ride to the ranch, he had made awkward conversation about the weather and managed nothing more. At the ranch, he had spent all of his time with Tom Noonan and Joseph Woods, almost ignoring Mandy, who seemed content enough helping Ruth.

What was wrong with him?

'What's wrong, Mr Wilsey?'

'Excuse me?'

'You look worried, Mr Wilsey. I hope nothing is wrong.'

'No, of course not.' Phineas could tell his companion didn't believe him. He decided to tell the truth, if not exactly the most immediate truth. 'Well, I am concerned about today's *Grayson Herald*.'

'Why? The paper is ready to go. All we have to do is get copies over to Benson's Mercantile and, of course, sell it at the office.'

'Yes, but, you see, Miss Woods, the *Grayson Herald* has had it lucky so far.'

'What do you mean?'

'Well, because of, ah, fortuitous circumstances the paper has been able to print the truth without directly offending Leonard Caldwell and losing most of our advertisers.'

'Mr Caldwell is going to be plenty offended by the editorial you wrote for today's *Herald*.' There was a strong element of pride in Mandy's voice but her boss was too nervous to catch it.

'Yes, well, you see, I've never had to deal with a situation exactly like this one before and I—'

'Mr Wilsey, you have all the talents and instincts of a great journalist. You have already proven that with the bold stand you took while working in New York. I know you will do what is right and I am proud to be working with you at the *Herald*.'

Phineas was stunned. If he had been almost speechless before, he was now totally mute. He looked at his horse and began to pat him on the neck. After several repetitive pats the horse turned his head toward his rider as if asking what the fuss was all about.

The newspaper man swallowed and turned to his companion. 'Thank you, that means a lot. I, ah, am honored to have you as an editor, reporter and, well, it's just wonderful to have you around.'

'Why, thank you, Mr Wilsey.'

They rode the rest of the way in silence.

Deputy Harry Blackburn knew something strange was in the air the moment he spotted the crowd in front of the newspaper office. Yeah, Tuesday was one of the days the paper came out, and people stopped by the office to buy it, but this Tuesday was different. A dozen or so people were hanging around the *Herald* office, talking in an excited manner.

Although the crowd parted for him, Blackburn still made a point of shoving a few men aside as he entered the newspaper office. Inside, five more people were talking with Phineas Wilsey and the Woods girl. A stack of newspapers sat on a table. The deputy walked over and grabbed one.

'That will be two pennies, please,' Mandy Woods said politely.

'Don't lawmen get any special considerations in this town?' Blackburn snapped.

'The lawmen in this town get more than enough special considerations, Deputy Blackburn,' Phineas replied sharply. 'If you want a newspaper, you can pay for it just like anyone else.'

The crowd standing outside the office was silent now, all of them watching the minor drama being performed. This was not the place to make trouble and the deputy knew it. He tossed two pennies on the table and groused at Mandy. 'You was better off selling snake oil.'

As he walked angrily out of the office, Harry Blackburn could hear restrained snickering coming from the crowd. He cursed loudly, not caring who heard him. That only led to a burst of laughter from the people gathered.

Blackburn walked quickly back to the sheriff's office. Lou Dixon wasn't there. No surprise. Dixon pretty much came and went as he pleased, leaving all the work to him.

The deputy sat at the office desk with the newspaper, anxious to find out what had everyone so all-fired excited. The first page consisted of stories about the murder of Stephen Hayworth. No surprise there. He kept reading until he came to the editorial page. Harry Blackburn suddenly understood the furor.

Common Sense and Common Decency.

The brutal murder of Stephen Hayworth is surrounded by all too familiar circumstances. Two men, both employed by Leonard Caldwell, claim to have witnessed the murder and have identified Ox Bentley as the killer.

Last Friday night, Tom Noonan criticized Leonard Caldwell for running people off their own property. That night, Tom's home was attacked by five thugs. Three of those men were gunned down before they could carry out their evil plans. All three were employed by Leonard Caldwell. Before he died, one of the men, Stacy Ellis, confessed to killing Sheriff Russ Jones and admitted that Leonard Caldwell had paid him to do it.

Evil does not observe proper etiquette. It is powerful and pervasive, but can be stopped by people with common sense and common decency. The citizens of Grayson must band together and demand honest law enforcement for our town. In the next several issues, this paper will discuss the specifics of how this town can be rid of a tyrant and once again become a place where law and order is respected.

Harry Blackburn gave a low whistle. He now had a good idea of where the boss had gone. Lou Dixon was probably riding out to the Caldwell ranch with a copy of the *Grayson Herald*. Tonight, there would certainly be an attack on the newspaper office.

The deputy laughed bitterly. Lou Dixon was a hardcase, but a predictable one. That Wilsey had a slick gunfighter on his side. The newspaper office would be guarded tonight as it had been on Sunday night. With a fight, they could probably burn it down, but it would cost lives. One thing was for certain: Lou Dixon would be alive and healthy tomorrow morning; Harry Blackburn couldn't be so sure about himself.

Blackburn got up from the desk and opened the door that led to the jail area. Ox was sleeping in his cell. Lou Dixon hadn't bothered to get one of the barflies, who occasionally worked as part-time deputy, to watch the office. Of course, both of the doors to the office were locked and it seemed unlikely that someone could break in during the day. Still, it was one more example of how Lou Dixon left all the details to him, not that there weren't already plenty of examples to choose from.

Blackburn closed the door and walked back to the desk, but he didn't sit down. A nervousness was overtaking him, a feeling that this latest move by the newspaper could be opening up a real chance for him.

Leonard Caldwell sure had seemed fed up with Lou Dixon the previous night. If he could show Caldwell that he, Harry Blackburn, could handle troublemakers better than Dixon, maybe he would get Dixon's job.

Those two fools who ran the newspaper were birds that could be shot out of the sky. Oh sure, they had people laughing at him just a few minutes ago. But Harry Blackburn would get the last laugh.

A plan began to formulate in the deputy's mind, a plan that would make Leonard Caldwell take note of who could really get a job done right.

He was smiling as he left the sheriff's office. First, he would hustle over to the Mule Kick and get one of the barflies to watch the office. Then, there would be only a few more stops before he would make his move and, for the first time in his life, be hauling in some real money.

His smile grew broader as he thought about the next few hours: hours that would make him a rich man.

CHAPTER SIXTEEN

A sense of excitement pervaded the office of the *Grayson Herald*. Tuesday's edition was a sell-out and there was a chance that Thursday's paper would change the town forever.

Mandy and Phineas were busy putting things in order before they locked the place up and kept an important appointment. As he watched his assistant scurrying about, Phineas's excitement became tempered by concern.

'Miss Woods, perhaps I should go by myself. This situation could become dangerous and I would never forgive myself if something were to happen to you.'

Mandy bent over a desk and began to rearrange a stack of papers that she had just finished arranging. She wanted to keep her face down to cover her embarrassment; pleased embarrassment, but embarrassment nonetheless. 'I appreciate your concern, Mr Wilsey, but Harry Blackburn was very specific. He wanted both of us there. You are to listen to his story and ask questions; I am expected to record everything.'

As she shuffled the papers, Mandy mused over the odd circumstances Blackburn had insisted upon. They were to meet him at three in the afternoon inside an abandoned building. The deputy had claimed he would give them information that would send both Lou Dixon and Leonard Caldwell to prison.

And he could back up the accusations with proof.

But why not just tell the story and turn over the proof in the newspaper office? Harry Blackburn had been vague in answering that question. Something about needing total privacy. It didn't make much sense to her.

Mandy blurted out a sudden thought. 'Maybe we should talk this over with Reverend Colt. He may want to accompany us.'

A hurt look waved across Phineas's face. 'I hate to bother him. The man was up all night, told me he was looking forward to some sleep. Of course, if you feel—'

Mandy realized she had injured the young man's feelings. He had taken her statement as an indication that she thought he could not protect her. Mandy Woods did not feel that way at all. 'You are right, Mr Wilsey. Besides, there is a good reason why we should handle this matter ourselves.'

The hurt on Phineas's face turned to curiosity. 'What's that?'

'Reverend Colt is a fine man,' Mandy answered. 'But he will soon be moving on. Those of us who live and work in this town must take responsibility for it.'

Those of us who live and work. . . . The newspaper man was now beginning to feel giddy. He had been wondering, no, worrying over the wrecked box wagon that now sat behind the livery. He had hoped Mandy Woods's association with the paper would squelch Caldwell's promise to have the wagon fixed. He had been afraid to ask the woman about it, but now. . . .

Maybe she didn't plan on going back to *Brother Joseph's Traveling Wonders.* Maybe. . . . Ever since their awkward conversation that morning while riding back into town, Phineas had noticed that there seemed to be a new closeness between Mandy Woods and himself. He certainly wanted to do everything he could to encourage that closeness.

'You are absolutely correct, Miss Woods!' His voice was much more pontifical than he had intended. 'We must be responsible.'

114

He wanted to elaborate and present some specifics on acting responsibly but couldn't think of anything so he settled for checking his pocket watch. 'It is almost three, we should be going.' Well, he thought, being on time was a part of responsible behavior.

As the couple left the newspaper office, Phineas noted that the town appeared deserted. No surprise there. The afternoon heat was intense and everybody was staying out of it. He wondered, uneasily, if that was the reason Harry Blackburn had chosen mid-afternoon as a time to meet with them.

Summer days can be cruel, the newspaper man thought. The harsh light and heat made the buildings look more dilapidated, the streaks on the windows standing out like open wounds. The main street of Grayson looked fragile, as if the heat pressing down on it might wither everything to dust.

Phineas glanced at his companion and realized she was having similar thoughts. He wanted to say something comforting but no words of comfort came to mind as they drew nearer to the rotting structure at the very end of the street. A battered, crooked sign on the small building read, 'Yancey's Hardware'.

'Funny thing about that old store.' Mandy's voice no longer sounded as confident as it had back in the newspaper office. 'Father and I have made stops in Grayson for more than two years now. Yancey's Hardware has never been open. It's just always been an empty shell.'

'I don't know of anyone in town named Yancey.' Phineas spoke as the two began to walk around to the back of the former hardware store, following the instructions Harry Blackburn had given. 'I guess . . . well . . . I guess it really doesn't make any difference where Yancey is now.'

The couple exchanged tense smiles as they approached the back door of the building.

'Why do you think Harry Blackburn was so insistent that we

come in through the back?'

Phineas could think of several answers to his companion's question, none of them reassuring. As he opened the door, he wished he had taken Mandy's advice about Reverend Colt. He suddenly realized it wasn't too late. They could both turn and leave right now, but for some reason he just couldn't do that.

Inside, Yancey's Hardware was dark, the air heavy with a combination of bad odors. A scratchy sound of running mice greeted their entrance. Phineas glanced at the roaches on the wall. 'This is a place where rats and insects battle for territory.'

Erratic light was provided by sunbeams, which shot through the boarded-up window and a few gaps in the rotting wood. Phineas eyed the dusty shelves that lined the two long walls in the room. 'This must have been a storage room.' He nodded toward an open doorway. 'And that's where the actual business of the store took place.'

'I guess Harry Blackburn isn't here yet,' Mandy said.

'You guess wrong, lady.' Blackburn walked through the open doorway.

'I'm sorry, Mr Blackburn, we should have looked in the next room.' Phineas had been startled by Blackburn's sudden entrance, but tried to camouflage it with a casual demeanor.

'There doesn't seem to be any table or chair here, but don't worry, Deputy, I can write while standing.' Mandy held up a tablet that she carried in her right hand.

'Write what?' Blackburn's voice was low and contemptuous.

'Why, remember, you wanted me to write down everything you told Mr Wilsey.'

Blackburn gave Mandy a leering smile. 'Oh yeah.'

Both Mandy and Phineas were spooked by the behavior of Harry Blackburn. 'Deputy Blackburn.' Phineas tried to keep the fear from his voice. 'There is no need to have our meeting in this filthy place. It's so dark in here Miss Woods will have trouble writing—'

'Well now, if the darkness bothers you, just open up a window.' Harry Blackburn gestured toward the window only a few feet away on a side wall.

That suggestion caused Mandy and Phineas to relax somewhat. 'That wouldn't bother you?' Phineas asked.

'No. Just pull on the wood, it'll come right off.'

Phineas Wilsey had just turned toward the window when he felt an explosion against the side of his head. As he hit the floor, he heard a muffled scream followed by, 'Be quiet or I'll kill you right here – him too.'

The newspaper man struggled to remain conscious. He had to do everything he could to help Mandy Woods. As the room swirled around him, he forced himself to stand up. Staring straight ahead he saw, in a blur, Harry Blackburn standing behind Mandy, his hand firmly covering her mouth and clamping her head against his chest. In his other hand was a gun. The terrifying picture oozed in and out of focus.

'What's wrong, Wilsey, not feeling so good?'

Phineas felt like his head was splitting open. He lost consciousness before he could even hear the deputy's laughter. The newspaper man felt nothing as, for a second time, he hit the floor.

CHAPTER SEVENTEEN

Phineas again struggled to his feet. He sensed immediately that he was alone but still shouted, 'Miss Woods!' as loudly as he could. He stumbled around the former store but could not find any clue as to where Mandy had been taken.

A sense of rage overwhelmed him: rage at himself for allowing the woman to enter such a dangerous situation. How could he have been such a fool?

He grabbed his hat from the floor and placed it against the side of his head to stop the bleeding. 'I have to move fast, she's in trouble.' Staggering from the old building, he moved quickly toward the sheriff's office and barged in.

The man who sat at the sheriff's desk was a lout who looked strange without a drink in front of him. Phineas didn't remember the man's name and didn't care. 'I need to see Harry Blackburn.'

'Ain't here,' Amos replied.

'Where is he?'

'Don't know.'

Phineas grabbed the barfly by the collar and shook him. 'I asked you where Blackburn is!'

'I tell you, I don't know!'

Phineas stared at the pathetic excuse for a human being and

became convinced he was telling the truth. Wilsey pushed the saddletramp back into his chair, then turned and quickly exited the sheriff's office. He needed help and there was only one place where he could get it.

A loud pounding wakened Paul Colten from a nightmare. The horrible dream vanished from his mind the moment his eyes opened, but he knew it had been a nightmare. Nightmares always accompanied his sleeping.

The pounding sounded again. Colt did a quick assessment of himself. He had fallen asleep with his clothes on. He grabbed his .45 from the holster folded around a bedpost and approached the door in socked feet.

He opened the door a crack and then threw it open to allow Phineas to stumble inside. One look at the reporter told Colt there was serious trouble. 'What happened?'

'Miss Woods is gone!' Phineas's voice was a near shout. 'That snake Harry Blackburn has taken her and it's all my fault.'

'Calm down.' The gunman's words were a firm order. 'Start from the beginning, tell me the whole story.'

As he listened to Phineas's account of what happened, Colt experienced an all too familiar anguish. Two naïve young people got in over their heads and now the woman was in serious danger. The former clergyman inhaled deeply and concentrated on the crisis at hand. This was no time to think about the past.

'There's a good chance that Miss Woods is safe at the moment.' Colt spoke as he sat on the bed and put his boots on.

'Why do you say that?'

'Because you're still alive.' Colt bolted up and began to strap on his holster. 'Blackburn could easily have killed you. That's not the plan. In order to get Miss Woods back, you're going to have to agree to let Leonard Caldwell control the *Grayson Herald*.'

119

'If that's what it takes, then I'll make that promise. Mandy Woods is more important than any newspaper.'

Colt gave his companion a harsh look, then nodded toward Phineas's head injury. 'You've been bleeding too much. It's affecting the way you think.'

'What do you mean?'

'Do you really think Miss Woods would truly be safe if you went along with such a plan? Blackburn grabbed her once; he could do it again. The two of you would be like scared puppies always nervous about not pleasing your master.'

'What can we do?' Phineas was a step away from a break-down.

Colt placed a hand on Phineas's right shoulder. This was no time to preach to the kid. 'First thing, we're getting you to a doctor.'

'No! Miss Woods needs—'

'Hold on. You're right. Miss Woods does need you, but you're not going to be of much help with your scalp bleeding. A quick patch-up will get you back into action.'

'But—'

'While you're doing that, I'm going to be asking questions around town. Harry Blackburn thinks he is in control right now. He will approach you with an offer when it suits him. Maybe we can surprise him.'

A look resembling thoughtfulness came into Phineas's eyes. 'OK. But I'm getting to the doc right now. I'll be rejoining you quickly. Where are you going to start asking questions?'

'The saloons, of course.'

After leaving Phineas at the doctor's office, Colt did a quick search for Harry Blackburn. Not finding the deputy, he fell back on the plan he had shared with Phineas Wilsey.

The gunfighter's first stop was the Lucky Aces. The crowd

was sparse, consisting of men playing cards and nursing drinks to escape the direct heat of the sun. Colt bought a few men some drinks and asked questions about Harry Blackburn. The answers gave him no help. Men grumbled about the local law doing nothing except Leonard Caldwell's bidding. People had been saying that for a long time. No one seemed to know what Blackburn was up to on that particular day. Colt left and headed for the Mule Kick.

The Mule Kick boasted a few more customers than the Lucky Aces, but not many. The mood inside was identical to that of the other saloon: surviving until the sun weakened. As he stepped toward the bar, Colt spotted Skeeter sitting alone at a back table with a bottle and a glass.

'Hello, George.' Colt addressed the bartender as he leaned against the bar.

'What'll it be?'

'A little information.' Colt jerked his thumb toward the back table. 'I thought Skeeter only got two drinks.'

'That was when Mr Hayworth owned the saloons. Leonard Caldwell owns this whole town now.' George didn't try to keep the bitterness from his voice. 'He doesn't care how much Skeeter drinks.'

Colt nodded his head. 'I thought that, most of the time, Skeeter tries to control his drinking.'

'Well, he has been, sort of, until today.'

The gunfighter's interest increased. 'What do you mean?'

'Skeeter came in, oh, over an hour ago and ordered a bottle of the most expensive stuff I've got.' George nodded in Skeeter's direction. 'He's been back there by himself ever since. Celebrating something, I guess.'

Colt gave the livery hand a careful look. 'For a man who is celebrating, he sure doesn't seem very happy.'

'You've got a point there.'

'Thanks, George.' Colt left the bar and headed for Skeeter's table.

'Hello, Reverent,' the hostler said. 'Sit down and join me.'

Colt sat down. Skeeter took a drink. There was one glass on the table. The invitation to 'join me' obviously extended only to conversation.

'You must be mighty sore with this old cuss right now, Reverent.'

'Why would I be angry with you, Skeeter?'

'A few nights ago, you took my side when those two toughs were rawhidin' me. You ran 'em off. Could have been dangerous. I sure know what the drink can do for a man with a gun in his hand. And now, I'm right back here.'

'They were just barflies, don't—'

'That's the hardest part.' Skeeter poured another drink. 'Knowin' there are folks who are tryin' to help. Folks who care, like Mr Hayworth. People I disappoint.' Skeeter started to raise his glass, then put it back down on the table. 'I tried to work good for Mr Hayworth and I did, most of the time. But then some temptation would come along, like today.'

Skeeter hurriedly downed the drink. Colt grabbed his left wrist before he could pour another. 'What temptation?'

'Well, ah. . . .'

'Skeeter, I need your help. A woman's life is at stake here. This temptation you just talked about, did it come from Harry Blackburn?'

The livery man nodded his head.

'Tell me what happened.'

'Harry gave me some money, lots of money. Well, enough to pay for this.' He nodded at the bottle.

'What did you have to do for the money, Skeeter?'

'Nothin'. Just stay away.'

'Come again.'

'Just stay away from the livery. That's what the deputy tol' me to do. Said he would tell me when it was OK to come back.' The stablehand started to laugh but it came out a sob. 'He didn't have to ask where he'd find me.'

'Thanks.' Colt bolted from the table and headed for the batwing doors.

'Reverent!'

Colt stopped at the doors and looked back.

'I've wasted a lot of my life, Reverent.' Skeeter continued his sobbing. 'I've hurt more 'n my share of people. Think there is any forgiveness for me?'

'Sorry, Skeeter. I can't handle those questions anymore.' Colt hastily pushed the two doors open and left.

CHAPTER EIGHTEEN

Reverend Colt moved quickly but cautiously as he neared Hayworth's livery. From inside came human voices mixed with the clomping of a horse's hoofs. 'Yeah, wish I didn't have to ride out this afternoon, in this heat, but that's the way it goes.'

'Guess so.'

'Say, where's Skeeter?'

'Ah, he's not feelin' well.'

'Yeah, I know all about Skeeter's sick spells.'

There was a burst of harsh laughter. Colt immediately stopped, then continued toward the livery feigning a casual manner. A buckskin exited with a rider who was already wiping perspiration from his forehead. The man he had been talking to remained inside.

When the rider was out of sight, Colt stepped close to the building but stayed clear of the open double door. Pausing beside the door, he quickly peered in.

There was one man inside the stable, who looked nothing like a stablehand. A gun was strapped around his waist and he was carrying a Henry. His back was to Colt. He seemed to be staring intensely through a back window.

Colt pulled away from the door and moved to the side of the livery where he could hear a loud voice approaching from the back. He quickly flattened himself against the side of the building and felt both tense and vulnerable. Tense because he sensed that danger was near. Vulnerable because it was broad daylight and he could be easily spotted.

Harry Blackburn hated the man walking beside him but had to pretend otherwise. Ollie was undependable and probably more than a little touched in the head. Lou Dixon had told his deputy to let Ollie out of jail the morning after Grayson's ten-year celebration. Since then, the saddletramp had stayed low and caused no real trouble. Still, Blackburn planned to run Ollie out of town for good once he became sheriff. Right now, though, the deputy needed him, much as he hated to admit it. He had been able to get Mitch to help with his scheme. Mitch was another saddletramp, but one who could stay sober and handle a gun well when there was the promise of money. Still, Harry Blackburn's plan for the girl required more than just two men and he had to settle for Ollie. There was little time for recruitment.

'So, you got the girlie hogtied in her daddy's busted wagon.' Ollie spoke in a boisterous manner.

'Keep it down!' Blackburn spoke in a loud whisper. They were walking behind the buildings of Grayson's Main Street, and Ollie's voice carried all too well.

They arrived behind the stable. Against the back wall was a wagon that the livery rented out. Several yards away from the stable stood a corral containing four horses that could be rented along with the wagon.

The scene would have appeared tranquil except for *Brother Joseph's Traveling Wonders*. The busted box wagon sat slightly tilted between the livery and the corral. So far, no work had been done on the contraption.

Harry pointed a thumb toward the wagon for rent. 'We'll

hitch that thing up, put the girl in the bed, toss a few heavy blankets over her and get her out of here. Mitch has the map of where to go. We're keeping her in a cave outside of town. Later tonight, the newspaper guy should be getting over his headache. I'll have a little talk with him about the future of the *Grayson Herald.*'

'Mind if I step inside the Brother Joe thing? That gal got my best friend killed. Kinda like to see her feelin' uncomfortable.'

Harry Blackburn didn't understand the full implications of what his new hire was saying. 'OK.' He motioned toward the window for Mitch to join him. 'We'll get the wagon hitched up. When you bring the girl out, keep a hand over her mouth. She's gagged, but that might not be enough. You'll have to hold her tight. She's got a lot of fight in her.'

'Don't worry 'bout that.' Ollie anxiously walked toward the box wagon and opened one of the two large back doors. As he stepped in, he saw Mandy Woods lying on the floor twisting her body in a futile effort to escape the ropes that bound her. When she saw the newcomer, a look of panic flared in her eyes.

Ollie closed the door. There was still enough light seeping in for him to see the girl. 'Well, hello there, sweet thang. You remember Ollie, don'tcha? You and me need to get reacquainted.'

He bent over and began to untie the girl's ankles. 'Yeah, this time you and me is gonna get to know each other real good.'

'Sure you don't want a drink?' George asked the man at the bar. 'Might help some.' He nodded at the bandage that covered part of Phineas Wilsey's head.

'I'm fine,' Wilsey replied in a clipped voice. 'Has Reverend Colt been in here?'

'Yeah. Just a short time ago. Talked some with Skeeter.'

Phineas took a quick look at Skeeter. The man was close to

passing out, not much chance of getting any information out of him.

'Could you hear what they were talking about, George?'

'Yeah. Something about Harry Blackburn telling Skeeter to stay away from the livery. Know that sounds strange, wha—'

'Thanks!' Phineas Wilsey ran outside the Mule Kick and headed for Hayworth's livery.

Colt moved stealthily along the side wall of the livery until he was once again near the front of the building. The gunman then leaned against the wall and braced himself. He could hear Mitch's footsteps approaching. Harry Blackburn's henchman would be coming around the corner of the stable to help his boss hitch the wagon.

The steps slowed and then stopped. Colt's eyes quickly spotted the reason why. He hadn't kept his whole body pressed tight enough against the wall; his right arm's shadow spread out across the dusty ground.

Colt sprang from the wall and attacked the henchman. A hard kick knocked Mitch's Henry out of his hands. Colt advanced on his opponent and delivered two hard punches to the head.

As Mitch went down, Colt twirled and saw Harry Blackburn standing at the back end of the livery, gun in hand. Colt drew his .45 and hit the ground as a bullet sailed inches over his head. He then squeezed off a shot, then rolled in front of the livery for cover. Harry Blackburn fired carelessly, the bullet scattering birds in a nearby tree. Blackburn remained in the back where Mandy was being held prisoner.

Colt buoyed to his feet and shouted, 'Toss me your gun, Mitch. Right now, or I'll shoot.'

Mitch slowly drew the six-gun out of his holster and tossed it toward Colt, but his eyes shifted to the Henry, which was now lying only a few feet away from him. In order to pick up the guns, Colt would have to venture away from the livery and Harry Blackburn would have a shot at him. The gunman figured it might be worth the risk. He needed to bring down Blackburn quickly in order to free Mandy.

Pounding footsteps caused the gunman to look behind him. 'What's going on?' Phineas shouted as he approached. While keeping an eye on Mitch, Colt gave the newspaper man a fast summary of the situation.

'I have to get to Miss Woods.' Phineas bolted toward the opposite side of the livery.

'Stop! Phineas!'

The young man didn't look back. He ran around the opposite corner of the stable, heading for the box wagon and Mandy Woods.

The gunman cursed himself. By shouting at Phineas, he had alerted Harry Blackburn. Phineas would be running into the crooked deputy's gunfire.

Mitch was poised to move for his rifle. Harry Blackburn was getting ready to shoot down Phineas Wilsey. Colt noisily stepped away from the stable and into the open as if he were trying to pick up Mitch's six-shooter. He then dived away from the building, knowing that Harry Blackburn would be expecting him to stay as close to cover as possible. Colt hoped the ruse would give him the valuable few seconds that he needed.

Her legs freed, Mandy Woods was using them as a weapon. One kick landed solidly against Ollie's mouth. The big man took a step back and ran a hand over his bleeding lip. The sight of blood on his fingers angered the thug. He looked down at the young woman on the floor and unleashed a string of obscenities.

Mandy replied through a gagged mouth. 'Unie . . aanhs!'

'I'm gonna leave your hands just like they are.' Ollie spoke slowly. 'That should make things a mite easier.'

Three shots sounded rapidly from outside the wagon, followed by a man's painful cry. 'Sounds like Blackburn,' Ollie said as he drew his gun and carefully opened one of the wagon's back doors, creating a wide crack. He immediately spotted Harry Blackburn lying still on the ground. 'That Reverend Colt must be around somewheres.'

Mandy took immediate advantage of the distraction. She struggled to her feet quietly, ducked under Ollie's arms and jumped from the wagon. Ollie was angered and then amused by the woman's escape. With her hands tied behind her back, Mandy hit the ground on her right side and stumbled twice as she attempted to get up. Once she was upright, panic caused her to run in a frantic manner, frequently stumbling over stones or her own feet.

'Too bad, sweet thang, you and I could have had some fun together!' The saddletramp raised his pistol and fired.

Ollie had not seen the blur which ran beside the box wagon and then headed toward the fleeing woman. Phineas Wilsey screamed as a hot pain seared through one leg but he managed to stay upright. Mandy Woods was not so lucky. When she turned to see what was behind her, she fell. Phineas dropped to the ground and shrouded her body with his.

Ollie jumped off the wagon and, gun still in hand, approached the fallen couple. 'Well, ain't this nice. You two get to enter the pearly gates together.'

Phineas pushed himself up with two hands and turned his head to face the approaching gunman. Mandy was lying face down beneath him. In the distance, he could hear the sounds of men fighting. It could only be Reverend Colt and the guy he called Mitch. Phineas knew that his life and Mandy's depended on the outcome of that battle. Meanwhile, he had to stall for time.

'Wait!' the newspaper man yelled at Ollie. 'Don't kill us. I will let you have it, every penny of it.'

'Every penny of what?' Ollie sounded cautious, but interested.

'The ransom money.'

'Ransom?'

'Didn't Blackburn tell you about the ransom he demanded for Miss Woods?'

'No, the weasel.'

Phineas spoke in an almost friendly manner as he nodded his head toward Harry Blackburn's corpse. 'The weasel got what was coming to him. Now, the money is all yours.'

'How much?'

Phineas knew he had to be cautious. The money had to be big but not so big as to make Ollie suspicious. 'Three hundred dollars,' the newspaper man said.

An intense, excited look beamed across Ollie's face. His words were shrill with greed as they piled out of his mouth. 'Do ya have it on ya?'

He never got an answer to the question. 'Drop the gun, Ollie!'

The saddletramp refused the command. He started to fire at Colt but was brought down by two bullets. A muffled scream from Mandy Woods punctuated Ollie's last moments on earth as he fell to the ground.

Phineas Wilsey rose to his feet, quickly freed Mandy's hands and untied the gag. Suddenly realizing that a gun lay near Ollie, he limped over and retrieved it. Looking back, he saw Colt, who had fired from a corner of the livery, checking to make sure that Harry Blackburn was dead.

Phineas stooped over Ollie and placed two fingers against the bottom of his neck. There was no pulse.

'I should feel sorry for him, but I don't.' Mandy Woods was

now on her feet staring down at the fallen gunman.

'No, Miss Woods, you shouldn't feel sorry.' Phineas spoke in a soft but firm voice. 'We are all better off now that this man is gone.'

'You saved my life, Mr Wilsey. Thank you.'

Phineas didn't know how to respond, but then he didn't have to; Mandy immediately began to ask about his leg as Colt ran up beside the two of them. Colt was able to establish that the bullet had only grazed Phineas but the wound was bleeding badly.

'I've already ruined my hat using it as a bandage,' Phineas said. 'Maybe I could tear—'

'Here.' Colt handed the newspaper man a thick handkerchief. Phineas tossed Ollie's gun to the ground and pressed the cloth against his left thigh.

'Miss Woods, could you help Phineas to get over to the doc's? I've got to take Mitch to the jail and, well, there's a lot of other things that have to be done.'

'Of course, Reverend Colt. I'll take care of Mr Wilsey.'

Colt smiled warmly. 'Grayson, Texas may not realize it yet but the town is fortunate to have the two of you here.' He gave a quick salute and then ran back to the side of the livery where a semi-conscious Mitch was moaning in the dust.

'I wish I could run.' Phineas looked despondently at his leg.

'You will be able to soon enough,' Mandy replied hastily. 'But first you have to get to the doctor.' She lifted his right arm and put it around her neck. 'We need to move slow, but not too slow. You're losing blood.'

'Miss Woods, I think I can get there on my own.'

'Walk.' The couple began moving at a reasonably fast clip.

'I hate to make you do this, Miss Woods.'

'Why?'

'Well, you know how grouchy Doc Cranston can be at times. He's always complaining about Easterners who come out here and give the West a bad name. This is the second time I've had to see him today.'

Mandy slowed their pace as they came to the corner of the livery, but as they rounded the building she saw that Mitch was gone, as Reverend Colt had promised. The young woman spoke as they again began to walk quickly. 'Doc should be honored to help you, Mr Wilsey. You're a man who stood by his principles, even though it meant losing an important job in New York City, and—'

'Miss Woods, that story about the job in New York, it, well, it has gotten a bit exaggerated, and I have to take the blame for that.'

'Oh.'

They were now walking past the livery. Mandy's mind drifted briefly as she wondered how long the horses would have to go unattended.

'I've done more good work these last few days than I have done my whole life,' Phineas continued. 'You see, I came to Grayson because the town didn't have a paper. Leonard Caldwell heard about me and, well, pretty soon he was calling all the shots. That has changed now, and I've never been more pleased. I really like it. I mean, I know I can build the *Grayson Herald* into something fine.'

'I'm sure you can.'

'Not alone, however. Miss Woods, you are what has inspired me to do all the right things. I couldn't—'

'Thank you, Mr Wilsey, but I know you would have done the right thing without help from me or anyone else.'

'Miss Woods, you mean so much to the newspaper and to me and, what I mean is . . . Miss Woods, will you marry me?'

Mandy Woods stopped and looked at her companion, her face reflecting confusion and shock. Phineas also looked shocked as if bewildered by his own question. But not for long.

The newspaper man's face morphed into a look of solid conviction. He nodded his head, confirming that he had meant what he had just said.

Mandy looked away momentarily. When she turned back, tears were starting to reflect sunlight at the corners of her eyes. 'Oh yes, I would be proud to become Mrs Phineas Wilsey.'

Phineas was shocked once again, but for an entirely different reason. Mrs Phineas Wilsey! The way she spoke those words! They sounded like music, beautiful music! How could he ever have been embarrassed by his name?

'You've made me very happy, Miss Woods. There is something else I need to ask you.'

'Yes?'

'Well, given what we have just talked about and everything, would it be all right if I called you by your first name?'

Although the question had been asked seriously, the couple suddenly broke out into laughter, a laughter of absolute joy. 'I love you, Mandy,' the newspaper man declared loudly, calling the young lady by her first name for the first time.

Phineas kept the handkerchief pressed against his leg as he kissed his fiancée. He felt very light-headed but it had nothing to do with the loss of blood.

CHAPTER NINETEEN

Leonard Caldwell eyed the line shack. Men were probably inside, playing cards and waiting for the heat to let up. He thought to himself that he should stop by and talk to his ranchhands, see how things were going. Instead, he spurred his horse forward.

Caldwell had been taking more and more rides around his spread and learning less about the ranch and the men he had working on it. For the first time, he admitted to himself that these rides were a way of being alone and trying to rid himself of his terrible headaches. The headaches were now becoming an almost daily occurrence.

Today's headache was the worst of them all. He had to get out, no matter how bad the heat was, and try to bring it under control. The pain had started when he read the newspaper Lou Dixon had brought from town. How could that Wilsey kid write those things about him and even challenge his authority? Had Wilsey forgotten all he had done for him? Why, without Leonard Caldwell there never would have been a *Grayson Herald*.

But the newspaper didn't bring the only bad news. Dixon told him that people in Grayson were reading the paper and agreeing with it, and congratulating that fool kid for what he wrote. They were even asking him about what they could do to weaken the power of Leonard Caldwell!

He would stop all this tomfoolery and he would stop it soon, but first he needed to be alone. He needed to get away from the cattle and the people in order to enjoy the quiet parts of his property. Caldwell guided his horse into an undeveloped area of the ranch that he treasured for the solitude and tranquility it brought him. He rode toward a large hill that afforded him a great view of the Bar C, a view that often calmed his headaches. Maybe it would work today.

A mass of terrifying shrieks suddenly flooded the air. The cries were coming from the other side of the hill. Caldwell looked instinctively at the rifle in the boot of his saddle, then raked the sides of his sorrel. As the horse galloped up the hill, the rancher thought he heard a woman's voice trying to shout over the cries.

As he reached the crest of the hill, he could see a woman below running frantically about shouting the name 'Rose'.

'Jeannie!' he exclaimed, then called out, 'What is it, Jeannie, where is Rose?'

The woman didn't even turn her head to acknowledge Caldwell's question. With her back to the rancher, she continued to run about, flailing her arms and shouting for Rose. The chorus of shrieks that Caldwell had heard before grew louder, almost causing him to cover his ears, but there was no sign of where the cries were coming from.

Perspiration flowed down Caldwell's forehead and stung his eyes. He wanted to turn and ride away quickly but checked the impulse. 'Jeannie needs me, Rose is in trouble. . . .'

He rode down the hill and dismounted. The woman kept her back to the rancher as she continued her shouting.

'Don't ignore me, Jeannie. Please.' He ran toward his wife. 'Tell me what has happened to Rose.'

The woman stopped and turned around. Caldwell was stunned. Yes, this was Jeannie his wife, but this wasn't the woman in the portrait. This woman's face was contorted by hatred for Leonard Caldwell.

'Rose is gone!' she shouted. 'Rose has gone to be with the other children.'

'What other children?'

The woman continued to shout. 'How can you not know? Don't you hear them?!'

The shrieks became even louder. This time Caldwell did clap his hands over his ears. 'Yes, I can hear, but—'

'Those are the children you killed, Leonard Caldwell!'

'Jeannie, I never—'

'Liar! The Bowers had three children. How many others did you order to be killed?'

'No, Jeannie, please listen.'

The woman's eyes flamed with an even deeper hatred. 'No more lies! I know what kind of man you really are. Look at your hands!'

Caldwell slowly removed his hands from covering his ears and held them in front of him. They were covered with blood.

'No!' The rancher turned and ran toward his horse as the children's cries became unbearably loud. He stumbled and fell and then began to sob into the earth.

Caldwell did not know how long he lay there or how long he cried, but suddenly everything was quiet. He looked up and Jeannie was gone. His horse was grazing nearby.

He hastily got back on to his feet and brushed himself off. He looked about and again saw and heard no one. His body trembled, and despite the hot day he felt cold.

He looked down at his hands. Those marks, were they red dirt or bloodstains? He couldn't be sure.

136

CHAPTER TWENTY

Reverend Colt flung open the door of the sheriff's office and pushed Mitch inside. The outlaw stumbled, then fell, splayed out on the floor.

'We meet again, Amos,' Colt spoke to the barfly still sitting behind the desk.

'Yeah,' came the nervous reply.

'Get out of here or you'll get hurt, probably bad.' Colt's voice was matter of fact.

'Harry Blackburn tol' me ta—'

'Harry Blackburn is dead,' Colt cut him off. 'Leave now.'

Amos paused, but only for a second. He got up and hastily left the office.

Colt stepped behind the desk and after going through two drawers on the left-hand side, found a ring of keys in the top right-hand drawer. He strode over to Mitch, yanked him to his feet, and steered him into the jail area.

Ox was standing in his cell, a smile on his face. 'Thought I heard your voice out there, Reverend. I see ya brought me some company. Don't mean to complain, but the poor fella doesn't look like he's up to much in the way of conversation.'

Colt opened the cell door and pushed Mitch inside. This time, the outlaw managed to stay on his feet. He made his way to the cell's battered cot and collapsed on it.

'You're right, Ox. That gent isn't up to much in the way of scintillating talk. Guess you'll have to settle for me. Come on, you're getting out of here.'

Ox quickly stepped out of the jail cell and Colt locked it. Both men hurried into the office. Colt brought Ox up on everything that had happened as the former lawman found his gun and holster in the sheriff's desk and strapped it on.

'You recall the name of this here safecracker Caldwell has coming in on the train?' Ox asked.

'Ah, Beau. . . .'

'Beau Toomey.'

Colt nodded his head. 'That's the name.'

'Know him by reputation.' Ox spoke slowly as if trying to conjure up any pertinent facts. 'Beau is known for being a dandy – likes to dress fancy.'

'Is he really a good safecracker?'

'That's what folks say.' Ox shrugged his shoulders. 'Trouble is, no one has ever caught him at it. There are no wanted circulars out on the guy. We can't arrest him.'

'We don't want to arrest him,' came the quick reply.

'Whatcha got in mind?'

'We head out to the Bar C. Wait until Beau Toomey does his work. Hayworth's copy of his will is proof that Caldwell lied about being left the saloons and livery.'

Ox shrugged his shoulders once again. 'Yeah, but that's all it will prove. Caldwell can buy his way out of that one. The man will still be getting away with murder.'

'Not if we play it right.' Colt began to pace about the office. 'We have got to make a big show of it tonight, Ox. We need to get that will and then tell Caldwell and his henchmen that Harry Blackburn is dead and Mitch has told us everything in order to save himself from the noose.'

'That's what my mamma would have called a half-truth.'

'All it takes is for just one of Caldwell's hired guns to testify against him in court. Maybe Mitch really would do it, but we can't take that chance. Besides, we can't be sure what Mitch knows.'

'From what I understand, Mitch never actually worked for Caldwell. He's just a hardcase who's a mite better with a gun than most. All he'd know is what Harry Blackburn told him.'

'Hopefully, Leonard Caldwell and his bunch won't give that too much thought.'

Ox pushed his hat back on his head. 'Reverend, I don't mean to sound ungrateful to the man who busted me out of jail and everything, but all this commotion you're planning to make tonight at the Bar C, it's gonna be tough. Caldwell has a posse of gunslicks that work for him.'

Colt nodded his head in agreement. 'On our way to the ranch, I thought we'd stop at the Noonan place and get Joe Woods. That would improve the odds.'

'Guess so.' Ox's face reflected determination. 'And this is the first time there has been a real chance to bring Caldwell down. Let's get the job done!'

The two men stepped out of the office as Ox continued to speak. 'Utah Benson is keeping my horse in a corral behind his house. His place is that-a-way.' He pointed west.

'I've got my horse tied up in front of the newspaper office.'

'I'll meet you there.'

'There is one more thing I need to tell you, Ox.'

'What's that?'

'You were just talking about getting a job done. Well, there is another job I need to do tonight. The job I came to this town for.'

'And what might that be?'

'To kill a man.' Colt spoke those words in a near whisper. They couldn't be heard by the hidden figure across the street.

CHAPTER TWENTY-ONE

Lou Dixon stood alone in the train station, building a cigarette. There were a few other people there, but they gave the sheriff plenty of space. Dixon placed his tobacco pouch and papers back in his shirt pocket, then fired up his smoke. He saw the stationmaster give him a quick glance and then look away.

The old guy probably wanted to ask me about the shooting over at the livery, Dixon thought to himself as he inhaled on the cigarette. The sheriff exhaled a low, bitter laugh along with tobacco smoke. He didn't really know what had happened. That fool Harry Blackburn had managed to get himself killed and another worthless jasper, Ollie, besides. Dixon had spotted a few townsmen gathering up the bodies when he rode toward the livery after returning from Caldwell's ranch.

Dixon had turned his horse around quickly and ridden toward the sheriff's office. From a distance he could see Colt entering the office and dragging someone with him. The sheriff tied up his horse and spied on the office from across the street. Colt came back out with Ox Bentley. They both looked determined, but determined to do what?

Dixon walked outside the station on to the platform and

looked down the track. He saw and heard nothing. No train noises, anyway. From back in the station came fast whispers and a few giggles. People had been acting differently around him lately, ever since Ox Bentley stood on top of a bar and pointed a Bible in his direction the Sunday before.

Dixon didn't like that and he hadn't liked what he saw at the Bar C that afternoon. Yeah, Leonard Caldwell had always been sort of loco, but now the old coot seemed to be going really crazy. The old man had begun to babble something about Wilsey hurting the reputation of the Bar C and hurting the feelings of Jeannie and Rose. Who the devil were Jeannie and Rose?

Dixon watched his cigarette smoke dissipate into nothingness. He was holding a bad hand and couldn't bluff much longer. He would do as Leonard Caldwell told him. He'd bring Beau Toomey, the safecracker, to the Bar C. Dixon knew Toomey by reputation. If anyone could open that safe it was him.

A whistle sounded in the distance and this time when Dixon looked down the track, he could see a spot on the horizon growing quickly bigger. A tenseness grew inside him as he thought back on the instructions he had given Phil before leaving the Bar C.

'As soon as the safe is open, you and me take a step back and pull our guns. I threaten to take the will, maybe even arrest the old man, unless I'm paid good. Caldwell's own safe is a wall safe right there in the office and it always has a lot of cash in it; old Leonard is antsy about banks.'

Phil looked doubtful. 'Why not just rob him now?'

Caldwell had looked down at the ground for a moment, trying to think of a phony reason; but time was short and he had to settle for the truth. 'Caldwell doesn't trust me. Whenever I'm alone with the old man, he makes sure his cook, Donny, is

141

nearby. I just can't read that foreigner. He's, ah, strange. But Caldwell won't keep Donny all that close with Toomey and the other men around.'

To Dixon's surprise, Phil nodded his head in agreement. 'Know what you mean; that Donny spooks me, too. You ever seen the way he handles a knife?'

Lou ignored the question. 'Besides, Caldwell has a bug in his ear about that will. He wants it bad and I'm guessing the notion of having it snatched out of his hands will shake him up hard. He'll pay a lot to keep it. Have fresh horses ready for us. As soon as we get the money, we'll ride off fast. I'll lock the bunch of them in the office.'

'They'll break out in a few minutes.'

'A few minutes is all we'll need. You and me know this country better than any of the other jaspers working for Caldwell. They won't even try to track us at night.'

The locomotive had pulled into the station and the waiting people who had been quiet and withdrawn a few minutes earlier were now noisy and laughing as they bustled about the platform, greeting newly arrived friends and relatives. Dixon felt bitterly resentful. There was no one in any town that would be happy to see him. It wasn't fair.

'Good afternoon, Sheriff.'

Dixon turned to see a medium-sized man with a brown beard and a black, expensive suit. 'You must be Sheriff Dixon.' The newcomer nodded at the star on Dixon's vest.

'Yeah. Look, I'm not the kind of lawman that—'

'I'm sure I know what kind of lawman you are, Sheriff Dixon. Shall we get going? I have important work to do.'

Another fool was treating him like an idiot, laughing at him. Dixon wondered if he might kill Toomey before running off with Caldwell's money. It was a casual thought, but a pleasant one.

CHAPTER TWENTY-TWO

Doc Cranston opened the door of his house as he was slipping on his coat. He glared at one of the two men standing on his porch. 'I thought you were in jail!'

'I got some time off for good behavior,' Ox said.

The doc's glare tightened as his face crunched. 'Rubbish. You were probably boring everyone in earshot with your preaching, just like you do to me every Sunday.' The doc grimaced and then stepped back to allow his visitors to enter. 'Suppose you're here to see that newspaper fella.'

'How's he doing?' Colt asked as he closed the door behind him and quickly looked about the small hallway.

'Better than he deserves, the fool. I told him to go home and rest, he has a concussion. So, what does he do? He gets himself shot. Lucky for him, the bullet just grazed his leg. The fool! I tell you—'

'I know, Doc,' Ox cut in. 'It's the Easterners who come out here that give the West a bad name.'

The doctor snorted and threw his head back like a horse. 'He's in the living room now with that little singing gal.' Cranston jabbed his thumb in the direction of the door to the living room, then grabbed his bag off of a table in the hallway. 'You can visit him if you want; I've got more important things to do.'

'Where ya off to, Doc?' There was a touch of relief in Ox's voice. He liked Doc Cranston, but was happy to see him leave for a little while.

'The Jacksons'. Emily is having a baby in a few hours.'

'How can you be so sure?'

'Because Emily told me. This is her sixth. She has the hang of it by now.' Doc left the house with his usual steady but not too fast gait.

As the two men entered the living room they saw Phineas Wilsey lying on a sofa. Mandy was bent over him, holding a glass of water. Both Phineas and his fiancée gave startled shouts when they saw the newcomers. Mandy placed the glass on a side table, ran to Ox and gave him a quick embrace.

'When did you get out of jail?' Her voice quivered as she took a step back and looked at the big man.

'Reverend Colt broke me out. He's too cheap to pay bail.'

'What are you two doing here?' Phineas shouted out from the sofa.

'We came to check up on our town's newspaper editor,' Colt replied.

'I've got a minor concussion and have lost some blood. I have to rest here for a few hours but I'll be fine.' The newspaper man glanced at Mandy, who was now standing at his side. Both Colt and Ox noticed the glance and sensed a new closeness between the couple. Yeah, Phineas was going to be just fine.

'What are you going to do next?' Wilsey was always the journalist.

Colt explained about the will in the stolen safe that was now in Leonard Caldwell's office and the safecracker who was going to retrieve it. 'Ox and I are riding out to the Noonan place to get Mandy's father, then we are going to visit Leonard and get that will. It will prove Caldwell guilty of fraud and, we hope, be evidence that will help convict Caldwell of the murder of Stephen Hayworth.'

'Oh,' Wilsey groaned. 'I wish I could go with you; you're going to need troops.'

Colt pointed a finger at the newspaper man. 'You stay here in town. Grayson is going to be needing you and Miss Woods in the future. Ox, Joe and I can take care of tonight.'

Colt's reference to 'you and Miss Woods' pleased the young woman, but she let it pass without comment. 'Dad will be happy you are taking him with you. He feels he hasn't been much help to you and Ox.'

'He'll be plenty of help tonight. Meanwhile, you take good care of the patient.'

Mandy wanted to tell the two men that the patient was now her fiancé, that she and Phineas had already been talking about their future together operating the *Grayson Herald*. But somehow it seemed a tad awkward to bring the subject up with men about to go after a murderer who was surrounded by vicious henchmen.

The young woman smiled and settled for, 'I'll take good care of him.'

CHAPTER TWENTY-THREE

'Mr Toomey, you have been at this for almost a half-hour now!' Leonard Caldwell's voice boomed. 'I've paid you well and I expect—'

'Quiet!' Toomey's voice boomed even louder and sharper than Caldwell's.

The scene in Caldwell's office once again turned silent. Dixon knew Toomey was, in his own way, an artist. He'd have the safe open soon.

The sheriff quickly assessed the situation. Beau Toomey was crouched by the safe doing his work. Leonard Caldwell was nervously watching him. There was one henchman also in the office, a gunslick whose name Dixon hadn't even bothered to learn. And then there was him and Phil Varden.

Dixon quietly stepped through the open office door into the hallway. He couldn't hear any sounds coming from the kitchen, which was down the hall. Of course, Donny always did everything quiet like. He wished he knew where that guy was.

'The job is done, Mr Caldwell!' Toomey's words spurred Dixon back into the office. Everyone was looking at the safe and didn't notice when Dixon closed the office door.

'There's one more safe that is going to be opened tonight.' Lou Dixon drew his gun and nodded to Varden, who was standing on the opposite side of the room, to do the same thing.

'What do you mean?' Caldwell looked incredulous.

'Open the wall safe, Mr Caldwell. The one right under that pretty painting of the mountains. Phil and me is taking everything that's inside it.'

'You can't—'

'Yes I can! Those papers in Hayworth's safe prove you're a crook, Mr Caldwell. And I'm still the Sheriff of Grayson, Texas.'

'You're nothing but a—'

'I know what I am. I don't need your opinion. Now get busy, unless you want to hand me that will.'

From the edge of his vision, Dixon saw the nameless henchman go for his gun. With a gesture that was almost casual, the crooked lawman turned his right hand and fired three bullets into the gunslick, who staggered backwards, then dropped to the floor near a side wall.

'That's blood all over your nice rug, Mr Caldwell. Too bad. You'd better move quick. Don't want any more stains. I'd hate to have to smoke you, too, and make Toomey here open your safe.'

As Caldwell took down the painting and began to open the wall safe, Dixon kept a careful eye on Beau Toomey. The safe-cracker looked bored and irritated, like a man waiting for a late train.

Leonard Caldwell opened his safe. Phil Varden emptied the contents into a pair of saddle-bags while Dixon picked up the office keys from the rancher's desk.

'Don't try to follow us!' Dixon said as he and Varden moved toward the office door.

'Why would I do that?' Those were the first words Beau Toomey had spoken since Dixon pulled his gun.

Dixon and Varden stepped outside of the office and locked the door. Dixon stood still for a moment. 'That Donny character doesn't seem to be around.' The two men ran through the front door and onto the enclosed porch of the ranch house. They briskly stepped off the porch to untie their horses from the hitch rail.

'Stop right there, both of you!' Colt stepped into view from the side of the ranch house, pistol in hand.

'Well, well, Reverend Colt, I guess we both knew this day would come.' Like Colt, Dixon held a revolver in his right hand. He now pointed the gun directly at Colt.

'Yes, but I wasn't sure at first.'

'Whaddya mean?'

'You change your name a lot, Lou. It took a telegram to the sheriff in Dallas to make sure you're the man I'm after.'

'After for what?'

'Bank robbery. Eight months ago. You killed a deputy sheriff. His family hired me to bring you in – or kill you.'

'How will this family know you've done the job?' There was a light coming from a window in the ranch house and a lantern hanging over the porch. Dixon stepped away from the house, putting his gun hand in almost total darkness.

Ox and Joe Woods stood far behind Colt, both carrying Henrys. Joe had his back to the scene. The gunshot inside the Caldwell house had roused the men in the bunkhouse, but they were being cautious. Joe could spot shadows moving around the storage shed, several yards away.

Ox kept his eyes on Phil Varden, who had a Remington .44 in one hand and the saddle-bags containing money from the safe in the other. Phil was distancing himself from Dixon and seemed to be preparing to fire if Colt took down his partner. The horses tied at the hitch rail behind them sensed the tension and neighed nervously while pulling at their tethers.

By contrast, Colt's voice sounded amicable and relaxed. 'Lou, I promised the family I would send them a picture of you, either in jail or in a pine box. Which way is up to you.'

Lou whistled and shook his head. 'A picture, huh? Times do change. Use ta be a gunfighter was expected to bring back the head of a man he killed.'

'Yeah, Lou, it's true what they say. Civilization is coming to the West.' Colt took a few steps toward his adversary.

'Guess I'd rather have my picture taken in a jail. . . .'

Colt heard Dixon inhale deeply and fired his first shot as Dixon squeezed the trigger of his gun. The crooked lawman twirled as Colt hit the dirt and fired a second shot, which knocked Dixon to the ground.

Phil Varden didn't even get a shot off before Ox's Henry took him down. Colt scrambled back on to his feet as Joe Woods fired at a group of men who were now rushing at them from the storage shed.

'Behind us!' Joe yelled.

In the dark, it was hard to get the exact number, but about a half-dozen shadows were now dispersing into a semi-circle, firing at the three men as they advanced. Joe Woods took down one of them, but Colt and Ox had been staring into the lighted area near the porch and their eyes could not adjust immediately to the almost total darkness. Their first shots missed.

A rifle shot sounded from somewhere near the back of the ranch house. One of the shadows went down and the others seemed overcome by panic; they turned around, or stood still, or fired at a target they couldn't see.

Colt's next shot took out another shadow. Joe and Ox both came close to their targets. The remaining shadows turned and ran toward the bunkhouse and the corral where their horses were kept. Colt, Joe and Ox fired in their general direction.

The three men grouped together, staring into the darkness.

'I think those hired guns have figured out they weren't bein' paid enough,' Ox said. 'We'll be hearin' the sound of hoofbeats pretty soon.' He stared directly at Colt. 'Looks like the last shot Lou Dixon ever fired was a complete miss.'

Colt nodded his head and then spoke as he began to reload. 'Someone was helping us. Wonder who?'

'Don't know.' Joe laughed softly as the sound of hoofbeats began to fill the air. Ox's prediction was coming true, fast. One of the gunslicks must have had a horse already saddled.

'You three men, drop your guns, now. I have a double-barreled shotgun pointed right at you.'

'Leonard, I know you've paid to have many a man killed,' Ox said. 'Not to mention the women and kids, but are ya sure you could actually pull the trigger yourself?'

Caldwell's footsteps could be heard coming off the porch and approaching the three men, who still had their backs to him. 'You men are my enemies. I will gladly pull this trigger. Put your guns down and then very slowly turn around.'

Ox looked at his two companions and signaled with his facial expression that they should do as they were told. They tossed down their guns. As the three men turned around, they saw that Leonard Caldwell not only had a shotgun in his hand, but there was a Peacemaker tucked into his belt, too.

'Now, before you die, you three are going to tell me the names of everyone involved.'

'Involved in what, Leonard?' Ox's question was sincere. He had never seen Caldwell's face so afire with hatred.

'In the plan to destroy me!' the rancher shouted. 'To destroy me and my family. You're not getting away with it. None of you!'

'Mr Caldwell.' The voice was soft and respectful, creating a strange contrast to Caldwell's insane bombast.

'Mr Caldwell,' Donny repeated as he walked between Colt and Joe Woods and stood in front of the three men.

'Yes, Donny, what is it?' Caldwell's entire body was shaking.

'Mr Caldwell, sorry I bother you, sir. Mr Caldwell, Jeannie and Rose here. Family need you.'

'My family. . . ?'

'Yes, sir,' Donny continued. 'Over there, you see?' He pointed to his right. 'Jeannie and Rose, you see them?'

'Yes, yes, of course, I see them.'

A stunned look burst over the face of Leonard Caldwell. His eyes bulged from a pain he didn't understand. The rancher never saw the knife protruding from his chest. He dropped to his knees and by the time his entire body collapsed on to the ground, he was dead.

The four men carefully but quickly approached the fallen rancher. Colt crouched over him and placed a hand on his wrist. 'Nothing. He's gone.' Colt spoke softly as he stood back up.

Donny stood facing the body in an erect posture. He said something in a language the others didn't understand as he bowed solemnly toward the dead man. Then he turned to the three men around him and spoke. 'Leonard Caldwell save my life. I repay him in only way possible. Mr Caldwell very proud man. Jail be terrible for him, public hanging worse. Quick death is kindness for him.'

'It was quick, all right.' Joe Woods's eyes widened as he spoke. 'I never even saw you throw the knife.'

'When did you realize what kind of man Leonard Caldwell was, Donny?' As Ox asked the question he realized that neither Colt nor Joe Woods knew the man who had just killed the rancher.

'At first, I see only man who save my life. Then he talk to picture of his dead wife and child. He say he going build big ranch in Texas for his wife and child. I feel very sad for him. In time, I see he have head sickness. He bring here many men,

151

they happy to kill. Why I not stop him before tonight? If I stop him, maybe some people not die. Good people not die.'

Colt saw the agony on Donny's face and moved to another topic. 'What are you going to do now?'

As they talked, more hoofbeats sounded in the distance along with cheerful shouts. More men were riding off and others were celebrating their departure.

'I talk to ranch-hands. Only real ranch-hands. Gunmen all gone now, I ask other men to stay. Mr Caldwell have brother in Arizona. Two years ago, Mr Caldwell not so sick. I hear Mr Caldwell talk to lawyer about will. Mr Caldwell say if he die, his brother will come to ranch and give to grown son. Son have wife and young child. I will stay here if son family want me.'

Donny looked down at the body of the man he had killed. 'Mr Ox, you do favor for me?'

'I wouldn't be standin' here right now, if not for that fast hand of yours. I guess it ain't askin' much for me to do ya a favor.'

'We bury Mr Caldwell here on ranch near his wife and child. Please, you read words over his grave? Mr Caldwell want bury in Christian way.'

'Sure.'

Joe Woods glanced around him. 'There are several men who will need burying here tonight.'

'No.' Donny's response was firm. 'You take other men to town. Bury men in town. Mr Caldwell not want them bury on ranch.'

Footsteps sounded from the front of the house; all four men turned and watched as Beau Toomey stepped off the porch and headed for the hitch rail. Instinctively, Joe Woods moved toward the safecracker with the other men following close behind him.

'Where are you heading with that horse, Mr Toomey?'

Beau smiled in a relaxed manner. 'You know my name, sir!'

'My friends told me you were in town. I move around a lot. I've seen you before, know your reputation.'

Toomey's smiled brightened. 'Then you know that I am not a man who breaks the law. I perform a valuable service as I did here tonight, when I opened a safe for Leonard Caldwell, who told me that he had forgotten the combination.'

'You're not a very curious gent, are you, Mr Toomey?' Joe ended his question with a smirk.

'I am a very trusting man, sir. I was paid to do a job and did it. Apparently, there were some circumstances of which I was unaware. Those matters seem to be settled now. I will be leaving.'

'What about the horse?' Woods asked.

'I will turn it in to the livery. Mr Caldwell rented it for me.'

'OK.' Joe Woods sounded resigned. 'I want you out of town by noon tomorrow.'

'Those are exactly my plans, sir.' Beau Toomey, with a grand gesture, touched his hat and nodded to the four men in front of him. He then mounted his horse and headed for town.

As they watched him ride off, Ox whispered to Colt. 'That's one fine man. He can sure be a help to our town.'

'Beau Toomey is a crook!'

'I wasn't talkin' about Toomey.'

CHAPTER TWENTY-FOUR

Reverend Colt stepped inside the Caldwell ranch house. Leonard Caldwell was buried, a Christian burial as Donny had requested. Colt knew it was time for him to get back to Grayson, but there was one more thing he felt compelled to do.

Colt approached the dining room slowly, as if enemies lurked there. He entered and stared at the portrait on the wall. For a moment he experienced a strange bond with Caldwell, a man whose whole life had been brutally maimed when a terrible disease took away the only two people he loved and treasured. Had Caldwell blamed God for the tragedy?

The rancher had retreated into a bizarre fantasy world where his wife and child still lived. Keeping that world alive drove him to destroy innocent people. The gentle man in the portrait had become a ruthless killer.

Colt looked away from the portrait. No, he wasn't like Caldwell. The people whose lives he ended needed to be killed. Colt looked again at the portrait and remembered those months when he had been tracking Jerry Blaine. At times, he had felt like Christina was by his side. There were nights when, sitting alone in the dying light of a camp fire, he thought he could hear her voice encouraging him on, telling him he was doing the right thing to bring down a man who would go on killing without a touch of remorse. After he had fired two bullets into Jerry Blaine, that voice went away.

Colt leaned against a wall and wondered what Christina would think of him now. Would she be proud of the way he brought down killers or would she be horrified by what he had become: a former preacher whose gun was now more important to him than his Bible?

Colt turned and strode rapidly from the house. As his fast footsteps hit the front porch, both Ox and Joe Woods looked at him curiously. 'Everythin' OK?' Ox asked.

Colt nodded his head as he stood between the two men.

Ox pointed a thumb toward a brush-covered hillside. 'The horses are still where we left them. Thought we'd get back to town.'

There was an unsettling silence. Colt said nothing.

Joe Woods broke the silence. 'Are you ready?'

Paul Colten, the man now called Reverend Colt, suddenly looked around him and gave a sad smile. 'Yes, I'm ready.'

CHAPTER
TWENTY-FIVE

The next day was a blur of activity. Donny's instructions were carried out. The bodies of Caldwell's hired guns were brought into town and buried. Phineas Wilsey was recovering quickly from his wounds and was able to take a picture of Lou Dixon's corpse for Colt to send to the family of the slain lawman.

When he went to bed that night, Colt realized he had spent his last full day in Grayson. He thought about leaving quietly at sunup but decided against it. He had a need to say farewell.

The gunfighter arose the next morning, checked out of the hotel, retrieved his horse from the livery, and rode to the office of the *Grayson Herald*, where he tethered the roan at the hitch rail. He approached the newspaper office hesitantly. Goodbyes were always difficult and this one even more so. He had come to very much like these citizens of Grayson, Texas.

Inside the office, folks glanced only briefly at the gunfighter. Attention was fixed on Mandy Woods, who was helping Ox with a tie.

'Hold still, Ox, and watch me carefully. You have to learn to do this yourself.'

'This is crazy, Miss Woods. Gettin' dressed up for a picnic.'

'But this is a special occasion, Ox. Today is your first day as the new mayor of Grayson.'

Colt looked in a stunned manner at Phineas Wilsey, who was leaning against a desk enjoying the spectacle before him. 'Yes, Ox Bently is our new mayor,' Phineas replied quietly to Colt's dropped jaw. 'Grayson has always had a town council, but it didn't amount to anything. Last night they met and appointed Ox our new mayor for three months, when elections will be held. It seems our former mayor, Horatio Camrose, left town in a hurry yesterday morning when he heard that Leonard Caldwell was dead.'

'I can't breathe, I can't breathe!' Ox's shouts filled the air.

'OK, I'll loosen the tie. Just hold still!' Mandy yanked at the item around Ox's neck.

'Shouldn't have surprised me.' Colt didn't try to keep the amusement from his voice. 'After all, Ox is now the town's most prominent businessman. He owns two saloons and the livery.'

'I doubt if anyone will even run against him. The same can be said for our new sheriff.' Phineas nodded at Joe Woods, who sat at a small desk near Ox and Mandy, trying to stifle his laughter.

'I saw Joe Woods in action two nights ago,' Colt said. 'He'll be an excellent sheriff.'

Colt reflected briefly on how the town had responded to the news of Leonard Caldwell's death. There had been shock, followed by a celebratory mood that led to the calling of a town picnic.

'Doesn't he look distinguished, Reverend Colt?' Mandy's question returned Colt to the present. He immediately agreed with the young woman.

Mandy continued, 'Ox, this is how I want you to dress when you preside at our wedding.'

Paul Colten smiled at both Mandy and Phineas. 'That news

doesn't surprise me, and it makes me very glad.'

Mandy looked at her fiancé as she spoke. 'We'll be setting a date as soon as we find out when Phineas's family can get here from New York.'

'And it's all gonna be proper!' Ox proclaimed. 'I've got me a preacher's license from the Methodist church.'

Colt's eyebrows went up a notch. 'I didn't know that.'

'Well, nobody thinks I preach very good; didn't think tellin' folks I was licensed and all would impress them much.'

'You're a fine preacher, Ox.' Mandy almost sounded like she was upbraiding the man. 'That sermon you delivered last Sunday changed this town forever.'

The young woman paused, looked at the people around her and then continued. 'What a time this has been. Last Sunday, everything seemed so wonderful. Then, Mr Hayworth was murdered and Ox arrested. We were in the deepest pit of Hades. Now, Leonard Caldwell is gone and this town seems reborn. We're having a picnic.'

'Don't forget our conversation about evil, Miss Woods.'

'I won't, Reverend Colt. You're a pretty good preacher yourself.'

There was a touch of light laughter, then Colt made a hurried goodbye, which was met with surprise. 'You have to come to the picnic,' Mandy declared. 'It starts in just a few minutes. We're having it mid-morning to get ahead of the heat.'

'Yeah,' the new sheriff spoke up. 'Ruth and Tom Noonan will be there. They want to thank you for everything. You know, they are going to make that contract with the army and you are part of the reason why.'

'I'd love to go, but I have to be on my way.' There was more to it than that, of course. Colt understood that Grayson, Texas was beginning a new day in its history, a time of order and decency. He no longer belonged. His stay in town had been a short but terrible time of violence and death. Grayson needed to move beyond that time.

Mandy Woods picked up a picnic basket and the entire group began to make their way out of the office as they wished Colt well. Outside on the boardwalk, Phineas paused to lock the door. The others began to walk toward the picnic area and Mandy walked with Colt to his horse.

'I guess I'm not going to write it.'

'Write what, Miss Woods?'

The young woman laughed softly and smiled at her companion. 'Remember, when I told you someday I would like to write your story?'

Colt nodded his head.

'Well, it doesn't look like I'm going to.' She gave Colt a wistful look, then continued, 'But I hope that down the road you will find someone you can trust with your story. I'll be praying for you, Reverend Colt.'

Colt touched his hat. 'Thank you, Miss Woods.'

Mandy stepped back to the boardwalk as Colt waved goodbye to Phineas. The gunfighter watched as Mandy and Phineas linked arms and began their walk to the picnic, their faces lighted by looks of joy.

Colt untied his roan, mounted and began to ride out of town. He then stopped his horse and turned around to view the scene on Grayson's Main Street. Mandy and Phineas seemed to be serving as magnets. People were joining with them in their walk. The crowd was becoming increasingly distant and Colt couldn't hear specific words, only the laughter and exclamations of merriment.

Reverend Colt patted his horse. 'I'm leaving this town in good hands.' He smiled as he rode off.